A COWARD'S REVENGE

But unknown to Slocum another danger lurked behind them. It was the man who had shown such interest in the Appaloosa, and later in Denver had taken a shine to Millie. Slocum had already had two chances to kill the man, and he had let him go the first time, believing him to be a coward and a bully. The second time, he had shot the man but not bothered to see if he had killed him.

The man bore a grudge. He was following them on the road. He did not want to ride in on Slocum in the daylight, even though it was already fading. Slocum was much too dangerous for that. When he met up with Slocum again, he meant for it to be a surprise. He meant to shoot Slocum in the back or while he was sleeping. He would get him this time. This time would be the last . . .

JAKE LOGAN

SLOCUM
AND THE
STOREKEEPER'S WIFE

JOVE BOOKS, NEW YORK

This is a work of fiction. Names, characters, places, and incidents
either are the product of the author's imagination or are used
fictitiously, and any resemblance to actual persons living or dead,
business establishments, events, or locales is entirely coincidental.

SLOCUM AND THE STOREKEEPER'S WIFE

A Jove Book / published by arrangement with
the author

PRINTING HISTORY
Jove edition / February 2004

ISBN: 0-515-13684-0

A JOVE BOOK®
Jove Books are published by The Berkley Publishing Group,
a division of Penguin Group (USA) Inc.,
375 Hudson Street, New York, New York 10014.
JOVE and the "J" design
are trademarks belonging to Penguin Group (USA) Inc.

PRINTED IN THE UNITED STATES OF AMERICA

10   9   8   7   6   5   4   3   2   1

1

The wagon rolled along the high mountain road at a leisurely pace toward the little town of Mesa Poquita. One grizzled old man sat on the box driving the two horses. Now and then he would snap his long whip over their heads and call out to them to move along. Another sat beside him holding a shotgun, a somewhat younger man, bearded and scruffy. The wagon bed was loaded down with something, but the contents were not apparent, having been covered over with a large canvas tarp and then tied down. The pull was uphill and slow, and just off to the left of the wagon was a sharp drop-off. The road was narrow, with barely room for a horse and rider to pass the wagon. To the right, the mountain rose even higher, and it was dotted sparsely with boulders and with clumps of brush.

Suddenly a shot rang out, and the shotgun rider slumped where he sat. The driver, instantly alert and in fear for his own life, whipped up the horses, and the body of the shotgun rider fell off the wagon, tipping over backward first onto the canvas, then rolling off the left side of the wagon. It bounced as it hit the road, but at last it lay still, dead. A second shot sounded in the stillness of the high hills, and the driver fell forward, his left boot hanging up under the seat for a moment, the top of his body dangling down between the wagon and horses. The horses were free to run, frightened by the two unexpected shots.

The dangling body bounced some more before the foot was finally released. It toppled down to the road to be run over by the wagon. The spooked horses ran on, faster and faster.

Ahead of them the road took a sharp turn. The horses made the curve all right, but the loaded wagon overturned, breaking loose from the singletree. It rolled over just to the edge of the road there by the drop-off. The horses ran on, dragging the harness and the broken singletree.

A few minutes later, two riders emerged riding single file from a narrow trail that ran on up the mountainside. One of the two men held a long gun in his hand. They moved out onto the road, stopping beside the fallen shotgun rider. One of the men dismounted and toed the body on over the edge. He stood watching until it hit the ground below. Then he remounted. They rode on, stopping again when they came to the mangled body of the driver. The same man dismounted again. This time, he bent to take hold of the body and dragged it to the far edge of the road. Then he tossed it over, again watching until it landed. He got back on his horse, and the two men rode together to where the wagon lay on its side close to the edge. This time both men dismounted. The rifleman shoved his weapon into its saddle boot. The two men walked to the wagon.

"There might be some good stuff in that load," said the one.

"Never mind about that," said the other. "We got our orders."

"Just seems a shame to waste it."

The two men put their shoulders to the wagon and shoved. They moaned out loud because of the weight. They shoved some more, and the wagon moved a bit. "Come on," said one of the men. They shoved again, and this time the wagon slipped over the edge. Both men watched as it banged against the wall and flew apart. At last, all pieces having settled somewhere, dust rising from below, they mounted their horses and rode toward Mesa Poquita.

• • •

It was later that same day when John Slocum came riding along the same road. He knew that Mesa Poquita was not far ahead, and he was anxious to get there. He had been on the trail for a long stretch, and he was ready for a rest. He had a little money in his jeans from his last job, enough to last for a few days of rest and fun. After it was gone, hell, he might look around for a job. He had not been to Mesa Poquita before, so he had no idea what to expect there. If there were no jobs, when the time came, he would just ride on to some other town. It made little difference to Slocum.

One town was pretty much like another. One job like another. There were some good people and a hell of a lot of bastards most places. Chasing cows on one ranch was much like chasing cows on any other ranch. He'd had so many jobs in so many different places that he couldn't even count them. Couldn't recall the names of all the men he'd worked for, the good ones and the bad ones. There were few places that were really memorable.

He'd hung his hat a time or two in towns or on ranches where he would have been content to settle, but in each case there had been some violence that he had been forced to take part in. Usually, he had settled the situation to his own satisfaction, but in the process he had done things to make the local folks, say, skeptical regarding his character and his motivations. Most folks thought of him as a gunfighter, and most folks were uncomfortable having a gunfighter around—unless he was on their side when they needed him.

As he rode along, he wondered casually what he would find at Mesa Poquita. He rounded a curve in the high country road, and then he saw two horses just standing there in the way. They wore harness, and they were dragging a piece of singletree. It did not look good. On closer inspection, Slocum could tell that the creatures had been running hard. He looked at the piece of tree they were dragging and could see that it was broken. Someone had met with an accident. Slocum looked to the edge of the road and frowned. This was not a good road on which to have a wreck. After studying the situation a little longer, he decided that the mishap must have occurred back behind him somewhere. He decided to take a look.

Turning his big Appaloosa, he began riding his backtrail. He rode slowly, studying the ground as he went. At last he came to a spot where large scrape marks showed at the edge of the road. He dismounted and walked to the edge. Looking over, he could see the broken pieces of a wagon and scattered goods of various kinds far below.

"Damn," he said.

It was a long and hard climb, but he made his way down to the wreckage. From the looks of the scattered goods, he decided that it must have been a wagonload of merchandise for a store. He saw where the singletree had broken, and he knew that he had found the wagon lost by the team of horses up on the road. He wandered out away from the wreck for a good ways in all directions, but he found no bodies. He wondered what had happened to the driver.

At last, he climbed back up to the road. He looked at the sun, low in the western sky. He would not have time to make a more extended search for the poor driver. He would just have to go on into town and report what he had found. They could send out a search party from there in the morning. He wondered for a moment if the driver could possibly still be alive. He puzzled for a bit, checking the sun once again and gauging the amount of daylight that he had left.

"Ah, what the hell?" he said out loud. He mounted his horse and started riding his backtrail again. This time he rode slowly, staying as close to the edge as he could with any degree of safety. It wasn't long before he spotted a body. It must be that of the driver, he told himself. Dismounting, he took his rope with him and made the treacherous descent again. He tied onto the body and managed to get it up to the road. Talking to his horse the whole time, he loaded the body on behind the saddle. Then he headed once more toward Mesa Poquita. When he came across the two draft horses again, he moved the carcass to the back of one of them. Then he led the team along behind him.

• • •

Riding into the strange town, Slocum gathered a small crowd in a hurry. One of the men was a deputy sheriff. It seemed as if everyone was talking at once, all of them asking questions. Pretty soon, though, the lawman shoved his way to the front of the crowd. He stepped up right in front of Slocum, who had by this time dismounted. There was something about the way the man puffed up and reared back that Slocum did not like.

"What you got here?" the deputy said.

The crowd had quieted a little by then.

"Two stray horses and a dead man," said Slocum. "Any fool can see that."

The deputy walked over to the corpse and lifted its head to get a look. He dropped it again. Then he turned to Slocum.

"All right," he said. "Let me start over. Where'd you come across them?"

"I'd say about seven miles out," Slocum said, pointing back behind himself. "I come on the horses first. Just like they are. I figured there must have a been a wreck, so I turned around and went back. This time I watched over the edge. I seen a wrecked wagon down there. It had been loaded with goods, like for a store, I'd say. Didn't find no human remains though. I went back up to the road and looked on back farther. Then I come across this fella. He's been shot in the back. Only thing I could figure, someone ambushed him, and the wagon got away."

"Hmm," said the deputy, scratching his head underneath his wide-brimmed hat. "Couple of you boys lay that feller out on the sidewalk."

Two men hurried up and dragged the body off the back of the horse, then laid it out so all could see.

"Anyone know him?" the lawman asked.

"I think I seen him a time or two," said one man. "I don't think he lives around here, though."

"I seen him drive a wagon into town before," said another.

"Any of you boys know if anyone was looking for some kind of delivery?" the deputy asked.

"Say, that's right," said a man in the crowd. "Larry Glover was. I was in the store just today with a list of stuff I need, and Larry was all out of most of it. He said he was looking for a wagon though, and it had ought to be in just anyday."

"Someone go find Larry," said the deputy.

A man at the back of the crowd went running off. The crowd continued jabbering. The lawman just leaned back puffing out his belly. In another couple of minutes, the man came back with another man running along beside him. When they had pushed their way to the front of the crowd, the deputy said, "Larry, do you know that there dead feller?"

The man called Larry stepped over beside the body and looked down at it with a long expression on his face.

"Yeah. It's Charley Jones. He'd have been driving my goods into town. Is that his team?"

"Likely," said the deputy. "This feller here says he found them out on the road."

Larry then walked over to Slocum and extended his right hand. "I'm obliged to you," he said. "My name's Larry Glover."

Slocum took the offered hand and shook it. "John Slocum," he said. "The wagon went over the edge. I found this man down there, too, but not in the same place. He's been shot in the back."

"Damn it," said Glover. "Old Bo Pearson would have been with him, too."

"You mean there's likely another body out there somewhere?" asked the deputy.

"That'd be my guess," said Glover. "Bo rode along shotgun—not that they expected any trouble."

"Well, they sure enough run into some this trip," said the deputy.

"We'll have to go out and look for Bo," said Glover.

"It'll have to wait till morning," said the deputy. "Too late in the day now."

"But—"

"The deputy's right, Glover," said Slocum. "It's treacherous down the side of that mountain. We wouldn't likely find him tonight. I'm sorry I didn't look further. I wasn't thinking about no shotgun rider."

"Don't apologize. You've done enough."

Slocum noticed that Glover was wearing a long face, but he thought that it was probably because of the loss of the two lives. The deputy sheriff ordered someone to go find the undertaker and someone else to take the two stray horses to the stable.

"I'll tell Elgie in the morning," he said. "He'll organize a search party, I reckon. Ain't much more we can do now."

He turned to walk away, as if his job had been done for the time. Slowly the crowd dispersed. Slocum looked around for a saloon. He, too, started to leave.

"Slocum?" said Glover.

Slocum looked back over his shoulder.

"Can I buy you a drink?"

"Why not?"

They walked, not to the nearest saloon, but to one a little farther down the street. It was called the Whistle Stop. Slocum hitched his horse to the rail, and they went inside. Larry Glover bought a bottle and took it with two glasses to a nearby table where he and Slocum sat down. Glover poured two drinks and shoved one over to Slocum. Slocum picked it up and emptied it. Glover refilled the glass. Then he took a sip from his own.

"Been riding far?" he asked.

"Far enough."

"Hell of a thing to come across at the end of a long trail," Glover said. Likely you're looking for a drink and a warm bed, and you come across a scene like that. I appreciate what you did."

"It wasn't nothing much," Slocum said. "I'm sorry I didn't find the other fella."

"Yeah. Well, we'll find him."

"It ain't none of my business, Glover," said Slocum, "but has someone got it in for you?"

Glover shook his head slowly. "Not that I know of. I can't think of any reason . . ."

His voice just kind of trailed off.

"I can't think of no reason a man would kill a driver and a shotgun rider just to wreck a wagon. It didn't look to me like anything had been took. If I was to have to take a guess, I'd say that he just shot the two of them and let the wagon wreck. That's all. The only reason I can think of is that someone has it in for you."

"I don't know who it could be."

Glover finished off his drink and poured another.

"You a storekeeper?" Slocum asked.

"Glover's Mercantile across the street."

Slocum finished his second drink, and Glover reached for the bottle. Slocum stopped him.

"I got to take care of my horse," he said. "Then I need to find myself a place to stay. I appreciate the drinks."

"Take your horse to the stable and come on back here," said Glover. "I've got a room in back of the store. It's all furnished and everything. I used to live in it before I got me a house. You're welcome to stay there."

Slocum hesitated a moment. "You sure?" he said.

"Sure."

"No strings?"

"None. It's just to show my appreciation."

"All right, Glover. You got a deal. I'll be back directly."

2

The room was nothing fancy, but it was decent enough. It might have been a storeroom, except that it had been furnished with a bed and a table and chair. There was a basin and a pitcher of water on a table standing against one wall, with a mirror hanging above it. Hooks on the wall provided places to hang a hat and a few clothes. Slocum did not need any more than that. He was more than content, especially as this was costing him no money. He slept well that night, waking early the next morning. The room had a back door to which Glover had given him a key, and he went out that way, hunting up a likely looking place for breakfast. When he was finished with his meal, he walked back out on the sidewalk. The deputy sheriff from the night before stepped right in his path.

"Sheriff wants to see you, Slocum," he said.

Slocum took a cigar out of his pocket and poked it in his mouth. Then he took out a match and struck it on the front wall of the eating place. He puffed at his cigar getting it lit. He had nothing to do, but he did not like the brusque way in which the deputy had accosted him. He straightened himself up from lighting his smoke, took a couple of deep draws on it and said, "Well, let's go then."

He walked alongside the deputy till they arrived at the sheriff's office. The deputy opened the door and stepped aside. Slocum walked on in, followed by the deputy. A man, obviously the sheriff, was sitting behind a big desk. He leaned back and looked up as Slocum stepped in. He looked from Slocum to the deputy.

"This the man?" he asked.

"Yes, sir."

The sheriff stood up and extended his hand. Slocum shook it.

"Your name John Slocum?"

"That's right."

"Pearly here tells me that you found poor ole Charley Jones out on the road last night."

"That's right."

"Well, I guess you heard last night that we got to go out there now and look for Bo Pearson. I'd like for you to ride along with us. Might make it easier for us to find him."

"Might I ask your name?" said Slocum.

"Oh, I'm sorry, Slocum. I'm Elgie Fletcher. I'm the sheriff here. My deputy there is Sammy Pearl. Everyone calls him Pearly. Will you ride out with us?"

"I'll go."

"Pearly, go out and round up a few boys. Not too many. No more than six. Tell Larry Glover, too. I imagine he'll want to ride along."

"I'll get saddled up," said Slocum.

"Meet us right back here in front of the office," said Fletcher.

In a few more minutes, they were riding back out on the trail Slocum had come in on. Slocum rode beside the sheriff at the head of the group. Just behind them rode Deputy Pearl and Larry Glover, and behind them six more cowboys, or would-be cowboys, Slocum thought. They came first to what was left of the wagon. Slocum rode to the edge of the trail and pointed it out. After everyone had a quick glance, Fletcher said, "It'll keep. Let's find Pearson." Slocum again led the way. He stopped once more when he came to the spot where he had found Charley Jones.

"He was down there about halfway," Slocum said. "I didn't know there was anyone else or I'd have looked more. But I was looking pretty careful from where the wagon is to here, so I'd say that Pearson is even farther on back."

"All right," said Fletcher. "Let's string out along here and ride slow. Everyone watch. We don't know for sure, but we think we're looking for a body."

Slocum figured that it wouldn't be far. If someone had ambushed the wagon and shot both men, he'd have shot one pretty quick after the other. He kept his mouth shut, though, and rode along quietly behind the sheriff. Pretty soon, Elgie Fletcher held up his hand as he halted his horse.

"I think we've found what we're looking for, boys," he said. "Everyone dismount."

Soon all the men were close to the edge, looking over at what appeared to be a body down below. It was farther down than the other one had been. Slocum figured that he had done his part. He'd just hang back and let someone else do the climbing and fetching this time. Fletcher picked out a couple of the younger cowhands and had them go down with their ropes. They went down slowly, tied around the body and signaled. A couple more men up above hauled it on up to the road. The two cowboys down below climbed back up slowly. In the meantime, Fletcher examined the corpse, front and back.

"Shot in the back," he said.

"Just like Charley," said Glover.

"Who'da ever done such a thing?" said a cowboy.

"Why?" said Glover. "Why'd he do it?"

"We'll do everything we can to find out, Larry," said Fletcher. "All right. Let's load him up and head on back."

At the site where the wagon went over, Fletcher sent Pearly and two other men on into town with the body, and he, himself, went down the mountainside with Glover to examine what was left. Glover was surprised to find that some of the merchandise was not badly damaged, but it was going to take some work to get it back up to the road again. Then he would have to bring another wagon out to the site and load the stuff up. He offered to pay a few of the cowboys if they would help get the stuff up to the road and loaded, and Slocum volunteered to go back to town for a wagon. They were all day loading the wagon. By the time they got it into town, it was dark. The cowboys were worn out and wanted to be paid, so Glover paid them off.

"Hell," said Glover, "I'll be all night unloading this stuff now."

"I'll give you a hand," said Slocum, feeling like he ought to do something for his board.

They were about to get started when a woman came out the front door of the store.

"I see you managed to save something from the wreck," she said.

"Yeah," said Glover. "More than I expected. Darling, this here is John Slocum. I told you about him. John, this is my wife, June."

Slocum removed his hat. "Pleased to meet you, ma'am," he said, and he noticed that June was a fine-looking woman. He thought casually that Larry Glover was a very lucky man indeed.

June stayed in the store while Slocum and Glover unloaded the wagon. She busied herself taking inventory and putting away the salvaged items as the men brought them in. It was late when they finished, and June excused herself to go home to bed. Glover offered to pay Slocum, but Slocum refused to take his money.

"Well, then, let me buy you another drink," Glover said.

"You don't want to get on home to that pretty wife?" said Slocum.

"It's all right," said Glover. "She'll be asleep anyhow. It's been a long day."

"All right then," Slocum said, and the two men walked back to the Whistle Stop, where Glover ordered a bottle and two glasses. They sat again at the same table. It was late enough that business had slowed down. As Glover poured two drinks, Slocum said, "Well, I hope you didn't lose too much on that deal."

"I lost enough," said Glover. "It hurt, but then, it could

have been a whole lot worse. I'd sure like to know who to blame it all on."

"I reckon the sheriff'll investigate," said Slocum.

"He'll try," said Glover. "Elgie's a good man. It don't look to me like he's got much to go on, though."

"You got no idea who might be behind this thing?"

"Not a damn one, Slocum. I've been wracking my brain, and I can't come up with nothing."

"I'd say it's someone who wants you out of business."

"Yeah, but I can't think who the hell it might be. I got no enemies that I know about."

"What about competition?"

Glover gave a shrug. "I got the only store in town."

"Anyone offer to buy you out lately?"

"No one's ever offered. Everyone in town seemed real happy when I put the store in a few years back. They'd had to order everything hauled in here till then or else make a trip out somewheres themselves."

They had a couple more drinks, and then Glover began to fade. "I got to go home to bed, Slocum," he said. "You can stay here and drink this stuff or carry it with you back to the room. It's paid for."

"Thanks, Glover. I reckon I'll carry it on over to the room."

Slocum took another slug of bourbon out of the bottle before settling down into bed. He was about to drop off to sleep when he heard a noise in the store. He sat up slowly and carefully, trying not to make any noise. He got his jeans and pulled them back on. Then he took his Colt out of the holster where it had been hanging on a peg on the wall. He moved cautiously to the door that led into the store and opened it very slowly, just enough to peek through.

There was no light in the store, and it took a moment for his eyes to adjust to seeing in the dark. First he noticed a movement. Then he could see that it was a man sneaking over close to the wall. There was a shelf against that wall, and Slocum thought that he could recall seeing jeans stacked there. The man seemed to be pouring something out on the stacked jeans.

"Hey, you there," said Slocum.

The man whirled, throwing something across the room at the voice. From the sound and the smell, Slocum figured that it was a can of coal oil. It missed him by several feet. The man ran for the front door, but Slocum was right behind him. He grabbed the man by the shirt collar. The man spun around, swinging a fist that knocked Slocum off balance. He quickly recovered and leveled the Colt.

"Stop or I'll blow you away," he said.

Just then everything went black.

He came to slowly and smelled smoke. It took him a few seconds to bring it all back into clear focus. Someone had started a fire. He came to his feet as quickly as he could. Looking around, he could see flames over at the shelf of jeans. He ran over there quickly and swept the burning garments off the shelf. Then he found a blanket, pulled it off the shelf and began beating at the flames. When he had them mostly under control, he went outside to a water trough with a bucket, and back in the store, he poured water over everything that was still smoldering. The fire was out, but considerable damage had been done. He tried to think what he should do next. Of course, Larry Glover should be notified, but he had no idea where Glover's house was. He stepped outside, still in his bare feet, and looked up and down the street. It was deserted. He wondered if anyone would be at the sheriff's office. *Well, hell,* he thought, *there's only one way to find out.*

He went back into his room and finished dressing. Then he went back through the store. This time he noticed that the front door had been broken into. He shut it and walked on down the street. He found the sheriff's office locked up, but squinting through the window, he could see Pearly asleep at the desk. He pounded on the door till Pearly woke up and came grumbling to open it. Pearly looked at Slocum through blurry eyes.

"What the hell do you want?" he asked, none too friendly.

"Someone just tried to burn Glover's store," said Slocum.

"What?"

"Someone just set a fire in Glover's store. I'd have gone for Glover, but I don't know where his house is."

"God damn," said Pearly. He wiped at his eyes, picked up his hat and followed Slocum back to the store. Slocum showed him the mess. "Let's go get Glover," Pearly said.

It wasn't far to Glover's house, but it did take a while to wake Glover up. When he heard what was wrong, he dressed quickly. June overheard and got herself ready, too. They were all back at the store in a hurry, and Glover lit a lamp so they could see better what damage had been done. Slocum had to tell them all what happened.

"There must have been two of them," he said, " 'cause when I threw down on the one I'd seen, something hit me from behind. If I hadn't woke up, I'd have been burned to death in here, and the whole store would be gone."

"If it wasn't clear before," Glover said, "it is now. Someone wants me out of business."

"Who the hell would want you out of business?" said Pearly.

"We been all over that," said Glover, "and can't come up with anyone."

"Slocum," Pearly said, "would you recognize the man you tussled with?"

Slocum shook his head. "It was too damn dark, and everything happened too fast," he said. "I got no idea what he looked like."

"They must not have known you was staying in my back room," Glover said.

"I reckon not," said Slocum.

"I'm sure glad that you were," said June. "Otherwise we'd have been wiped out."

"Well, I guess there's nothing more I can do here tonight," Pearly said. "I'll tell Elgie first thing when he comes around in the morning. Damn, that's two mornings in a row."

The deputy left the Glovers and Slocum standing in the

store surveying the damage. June started to try to straighten up.

"Don't bother with that right now," Glover said. "Go back home and get some sleep."

"I can't sleep now," she said. "I might as well work."

"Well, me, too, then," Glover said. "Slocum, we owe you thanks again. You might as well go on back to bed now, though."

"Aw, hell," Slocum said. "I'm wide awake. I'll give you all a hand."

3

They worked the night away cleaning up, and when they were done, Glover started trying to calculate his losses. June walked over by his side and put a hand on his shoulder.

"Larry," she said, "you've worked long enough. It's time to rest. That'll all keep for later. Come on home and go to bed."

"Hell, June," he said, "we have to open for business in a couple of hours."

"Can't you take a day off?" Slocum asked.

"Hell, we've already lost a bundle," Glover said. "We can't afford to lose any more."

Slocum realized that he had helped all he could. He decided that he was just in the way. He could have returned to the back room to sleep, but he felt guilty about that. Besides, he was hungry.

"Well, I think I'll go out and find some breakfast," he said. "Say, why don't you at least take a long enough break to join me?"

"Aw, I don't know," Glover said.

"Come on," said Slocum. "Both of you. You have to eat, and I'm buying."

Reluctantly, Glover agreed, and the three of them walked together outside and down the street to an eatery. They found an empty table and sat down. Several people spoke to the Glovers, expressing their sympathies for the late troubles. They ordered their breakfasts and drank coffee while they waited.

"Larry," said June, "who in the world could be behind all this?"

"I don't think we should talk about it now," said Glover. "Slocum don't want to hear any more about our problems."

"No," said Slocum. "That's all right. I'm kind of interested myself. Have you had any problems before?"

"No. That attack on the wagon was the first, and then last night," said Glover.

"Well, it seems to me like I've been involved from the start then."

"It's obvious that someone is trying to ruin us," June said.

"And you can't think of any reason why?" said Slocum.

"I been trying," Glover said. "Like I told you, we got no competition. I can't think of anyone we've made mad enough to do what they done."

"Well, there's got to be something," Slocum said. "Folks don't murder a wagon crew, wreck a wagon and try to burn down a store just to amuse themselves. There's someone somewhere with a reason for putting you out of business. We've got to find out who it is."

"We?" said Glover.

"I guess I've dealt myself in," said Slocum. *And,* he thought, *what kind of fool am I anyhow? I like to mind my own business. I ought to just ride out of this town and wander on somewhere else. I've got a little money in my jeans. Nothing's holding me here. Except I kind of like these folks, and someone's doing them dirty.* He lifted his cup and took another slurp of coffee. Just then a man, maybe fifty years old, walked in accompanied by a young woman, good-looking. As they passed by the table, the man spoke to Glover.

"Pat," said Glover. "Sit down and join us, won't you?"

"I don't want to intrude," said the man called Pat.

"Nonsense," said June. "We'd be pleased for your company."

"I'd like for you to meet John Slocum," Glover said.

"Slocum, this is Pat Patton and his lovely daughter, Patricia. Pat owns the Whistle Stop, where we had a drink last night."

Slocum stood up and nodded to the young woman. "It's a pleasure," he said. "I can excuse myself if you folks want some privacy."

"No, no," said Patton. "Sit down, Mr. Slocum. Shall we join them, Patricia?"

"I'd love to."

The Pattons sat down and soon ordered their meal. More coffee was poured all around. "I'm sorry to hear about the trouble you been having, Larry," said Patton. "What in the world's behind it all?"

Larry shook his head. "I don't know," he said.

"It's just awful," Patricia added.

"Do you have any ideas?" Patton asked.

"Not a one," Glover said. "We were just talking about that."

"We can't come up with anything," said June.

"How's your business been?" asked Patton.

"I can't complain about that," Glover said. "We weren't getting rich, but the last month has been the best we've had—till the wagon wreck and the fire."

"It's almost as if someone has been watching," said June, "and, just as it looked like we were going to get ahead, decided to knock us back down."

"We're not quitting though," Glover said. "Nobody's going to run us out of business. If I only knew who to fight, I'd show them some stuff."

"I'm sure you would," Patton said. "Well, if you get any ideas, I hope you'll let me know. Maybe I could help someway. You know, I could be next. Something that crazy, you never know what's on a person's mind. He could do anything. So what do you do from here?"

"I'm not sure," Glover said. "We needed that order. The one that got wrecked. I'll just have to place another order and bite the bullet till it gets here. I guess I'll have to tell the company what happened, and suggest that they put on an extra guard or something."

"Listen," said Patton, "if you need anything, you know,

a little loan or something, well, my business has been good lately, and I could—"

"No, thanks, Pat," Glover said. "We'll be all right."

"Just remember to call on me if you need anything."

"Thanks."

They finished their meals, paid the bill and left, the Pattons going their own way. Glover walked June back to the store and then went down the street to a lumberyard to order some material to make repairs on the store. Slocum made his own excuses and went to the stable for his Appaloosa. He saddled up and rode back out to where he had first encountered the loose horses. This time, he rode slowly, looking all around. He wasn't at all sure that the sheriff and his oaf of a deputy had made a good, thorough investigation. He found nothing more on the road, and he did not go down below to where the bodies and the wagon had been found. There wouldn't likely have been anything there. Instead, he went to where the bodies had most likely left the road. He tried to calculate where they had been when they had been shot, and when he had come reasonably close, he started looking up on the other side of the road. It took a little while, but he at last found a likely looking spot.

Leaving his horse in the road, Slocum began climbing up the side of the hill. It was a rough climb, and he loosened a few rocks along the way, but at last he made it. He found himself behind a large boulder in a nice flat place, a spot where one could settle down for a spell and be comfortable. He saw two spent shells and several cigarette butts. He picked them up and put them in his pocket. Then he sat and looked down at the road. He had a clear view. It would have been easy, picking off the shotgun rider and the driver from there. He looked around some more, but he found nothing else.

He then stood up and looked around. He did not think that the shooter, or shooters, had climbed up from the road. There had to be another way up there. The mountain rose a little higher, and he found the way up. As he started the climb, he could see that someone had used it before, and not too long ago. He was convinced that he had found the ambush spot and the way into it. At the top of the rise, he stopped, a little winded, to look around.

It was too far from town for a walk. There had to be a place to leave a horse, and there had to be another way out to this place from town. He couldn't see it, but he could see where it looked like someone might have gone down. He followed the trail down the backside of the mountain until he came to a flat, and there he could see that at least one horse had stayed for a while. He looked a little more. The shooter had mounted up and gone down the backside of the mountain on a trail that was not too steep. He followed it for a little ways, trying to figure where it might come out. He knew that it was too long a walk, and besides, his own horse was waiting in the road on the other side of the mountain. At last, he went back over the top, back down to the road, remounted his horse and rode back to town.

At the edge of town again, he turned and looked back to study the way the mountain lay. Then he turned his horse to ride toward the far side of the mountain. There was no road. He was riding across an open field. He rode for a while with no luck. At last, he went back to town and tied his horse in front of Glover's store. He walked on into the store, where he found Glover hard at work. June was waiting on a customer.

"I'm glad to see you've still got some business," he said to Glover.

Glover turned from his work to see Slocum. "Oh, yeah," he said. "Our customers have been pretty good to us."

"I just came from the ambush spot," said Slocum. "I went up the hill and found where the shooter laid in wait and did his shooting. His trail led on over the top of the mountain and down the backside. When I got back to town, I tried to find it, but I couldn't. Do you have any idea where that trail could come out?"

"Yeah," said Glover. "I got a pretty good idea, but it's on private property."

"Whose?"

"There's a ranch back there," Glover said. "It belongs

to a man named Sam Slater. He's a good customer of mine. I can ride out and show you if—"

"Can you tell me how to get there?"

"Well, yeah, I think I can."

"No sense in you riding out," Slocum said. "You're busy here, and I can look around by myself just as well anyhow."

Glover went to the counter and got a piece of paper and a pencil. He drew a quick map and then showed it to Slocum. Slocum tucked it into his pocket and went out again. He mounted the Appaloosa and headed back toward the edge of town where he had given up the search. Then he took out Glover's map and studied it. He tucked it back into his pocket and rode across the open prairie to the backside of the mountain. Then he saw a fence. He moved on over to the fence and stopped, looking both ways. There was no break in sight. He had to be on over the other side of the fence, though, and he did not want to ride all the way back down to the main gate. He would just as soon neither Slater nor any of his men see him anyway.

He turned the Appaloosa around and rode a good distance away from the barbed wire. Then he turned back to face it again. He patted the big horse on the neck. "It's a good jump, ole boy," he said, "but I know you can make it. Come on. Let's go." He straightened up, gave a little kick, and the horse took off fast. When they reached the fence, the Appaloosa rose up into the air and cleared it like it was nothing. In a few more strides, he slowed his pace, and Slocum leaned forward to pat him some more. "Good boy," he said. "Good for you."

He looked ahead to a grove of trees that was on Glover's map, and he made for that. On the other side of the grove, a stream was running along the bottom of the mountain, and Slocum moved across it and turned to his left. He rode along for a couple of miles, and then he saw the trail. It was narrow, but it wound up the side of the mountain at an easy angle. Slocum urged the Appaloosa up the trail. In a while, they arrived at the flat place Slocum had found before. He dismounted and left the horse, climbing on foot to the top of the mountain and down the other side to the ambush spot. He surveyed the road from there once again, looked around a little more and then went back to his waiting horse. He felt a certain amount of satisfaction.

Slocum had messed the day away. It was almost suppertime when he walked back into the store. He found June tallying up the day's receipts and Larry Glover laying his tools aside, getting ready for a break. He spoke to June, tipping his hat, then walked on over to stand beside Glover.

"You find anything?" Glover asked.

"Yeah," Slocum said. "Whoever did the shooting rode up that back way all right. Right off of Slater's ranch."

"You don't think that Slater—"

"No, I ain't jumping to no conclusions. I sneaked onto his place and rode up there myself. Anyone else could've done the same thing."

"But there's no question you found the place?"

Slocum reached into his pocket and pulled out the shells and the butts he had placed there earlier. Glover looked at them wide-eyed and then looked up at Slocum again.

"These were there," Slocum said. "He waited there long enough to smoke three cigarettes, and then he took two shots to kill the two men. When he was done, he went down the backside of the mountain and probably rode right back into town."

"Or stayed on the ranch," said Glover.

"He could have. The only clear tracks are up on that mountain trail."

"Those shells," said Glover, "they're about fifty caliber, ain't they?"

"I'd say fifty-two," Slocum said. "They're a mite unusual. It gives us something to go on. We're looking for a fella who rolls cigarettes and shoots a fifty-two-caliber rifle."

"He shouldn't be too hard to find," said Glover.

"If he's still around," Slocum said.

"What do you mean?"

"Could be someone paid him to do the jòb, and then he ran off. But let's just keep our eyes open for a while. What do you think about your sheriff?"

"Elgie? Why, he's all right. I think he's a good man."

"What about that deputy of his?"

"Oh. Well, that's a different case there. Pearly's just, well, hell, I guess he's all right. He's just awful puffed up, you know."

"I'd just as soon we keep all this information to ourselves for the time being, if you don't mind."

Glover gave Slocum a look of curiosity, but he just said, "Yeah. Sure, Slocum. Whatever you think."

4

At their invitation Slocum had breakfast at the Glovers' home. June did herself proud, fixing eggs, bacon, sausage, potatoes, biscuits and gravy. She had molasses and jelly available, too, as well as a large pot of fresh, hot coffee. Slocum ate till he could hold no more. Even so, he accepted a final cup of coffee.

"I wish you'd stay on and work for me, Slocum," Glover said. "The way things are going, well, I could sure use some help. I could use someone like you, too, someone who ain't going to run at the first sign of trouble."

"I think he means he'd like to hire a gunfighter," June said, "and we can't afford that."

"No, now that ain't what I meant at all," Glover said. "I just want someone who won't be scared off. That's all. Well, what do you say, Slocum?"

"Well, I—"

"I couldn't pay you much. Room and board. A small wage, say—"

"Hold it right there," said Slocum. "I'll hang around awhile for room and board. Let's just see what happens. Okay?"

"Yeah. Sure. Sure, Slocum. That's great."

June looked at Slocum over her husband's shoulder and smiled. "Thank you," she said.

"So what's our next move, boss?" Slocum asked. "I got nothing to go on except a fifty-two-caliber rifle. And I ain't seen anyone walking down the street with one lately."

"Likely whoever owns that gun keeps it locked up except for special occasions. I mean to keep the store open. That's for sure, but then, I don't reckon you're much for storekeeping."

"You may not believe me," said Slocum, "but I've done it."

"I've got a better idea for right now," said Glover. "After that wreck and then the fire in the store, I got to have me some more inventory in here right away."

"You got another wagon?" Slocum asked.

"No. I'll have to order one up in Denver. Along with everything else on my order."

"But who'll drive?" asked June.

Glover's mouth opened as if to answer, but he was interrupted by Slocum. "I will. But let's not tell anyone. Let's keep it quiet. I'll just ride out of here on my own horse like as if I was just wandering along on my way. If we're lucky, I'll get back in here with your goods before anyone catches on."

"I'll make out a list," Glover said.

"Do you need me for anything?" Slocum asked.

"Not just now," said Glover.

"In that case," Slocum said, "I think I'll wander the town a bit."

Slocum found his hat and put it on his head, tipping it to June as he headed for the door. "Thank you kindly for the meal," he said. "I ain't never had a better one."

On his way out, he thought again about what a lucky man Larry Glover was.

Slocum walked from the Glover house down the main street of the town. He saw the sheriff headed for his office, and he thought that it might be a good idea to catch up to him for a bit of conversation. "Fletcher," he called out.

Elgie Fletcher stopped in his tracks and turned to see who was calling his name. "Morning, Slocum," he said. "What's on your mind?" Slocum quickly caught up with the sheriff.

"Nothing in particular," he said. "I just saw you and thought I'd try to jaw a little with you."

"What about?"

"You made any progress yet on that business about Glover?"

"Not a damn thing," said Elgie. "Me and Pearly sat and went over in our minds anyone we could think of who might want to shut the Glovers down for any reason. You know, business competition, jealousy, something personal. Everything we could think of."

"Well?" said Slocum.

"Well what?"

"What did you come up with?"

"Nothing."

"Nothing?"

"Not a damn thing. Slocum, I can't find a reason in the world how come anyone would want to shut down the Glovers, and I can't think of a soul around who don't like them. It's a real damn puzzle, I can tell you."

"Well, I come up with something," said Slocum. He reached into his shirt pocket and pulled out the .52-caliber shell, holding it out for Fletcher to see. Fletcher took it and examined it.

"Fifty-two?" he said.

"That's what I'd call it."

"Where'd you come up with this?"

"I found the spot where the bushwhackers lay when they took out the wagon. Two of these was all that was laying there. Well, three cigarette butts."

"I'll be damned. You don't see many of these around."

"That's what I thought."

"Well, I'll keep my eyes open, and I'll ask around. Thanks, Slocum."

"Any time I can help, Sheriff."

Elgie Fletcher headed on for the sheriff's office, and Slocum turned and walked down to Pat Patton's Whistle Stop. It was early in the morning, but he found Patton inside preparing for the day.

"Slocum," said Patton. "It's a little early in the day for whiskey, ain't it?"

"Yeah. Even for me. You got any coffee on?"

"Sure. Sit down and I'll have a cup with you."

Slocum pulled out a chair and sat at a table as Patton poured two cups of coffee, then brought them over to the table. He put down the coffee and sat across from Slocum. "What's up?" he said.

"Oh, nothing much," Slocum said. "I just kind of wanted to go around and say my good-byes to folks I've met. I'm thinking about heading on out."

"So soon?"

"Well, I was traveling through when I hit town. There really ain't no reason for me to hang around. I'm feeling kind of sorry for ole Larry Glover, you know, what with all the trouble he's having, but I don't see nothing I can do about it. The sheriff's investigating."

"Yeah. It's too bad. Larry's a good guy, and his wife, June, is a fine lady, too. I just can't figure who'd be wanting to hurt them."

"That's what everyone says. Well, it's been a pleasure, Mr. Patton. Thanks for the coffee."

Slocum took his leave of Patton and walked back to Glover's store. There was no one in the store except Glover and June. "You got that list ready for me?" Slocum asked.

"Right here," said Glover, holding out a piece of paper for Slocum. Slocum took it and studied it. He folded it and tucked it in a pocket.

"The address is right there on the paper," Glover said. "I've ordered up a wagon and team, too. Ole Barns knows me. He'll recognize my writing. And here's a bank draft for everything I owe him. The last shipment and this one. It'll take you two weeks to make the trip. Be careful."

"You be careful right here," Slocum said. "Watch every move. Someone's trying hard to put you out of business. I'd hate to see them succeed."

"I expect, with what's happened, Elgie'll watch us pretty close. Don't worry about us. Just get back safe with all that stuff."

Slocum looked at the bank draft. He looked at Larry Glover. It occurred to him that this man was putting a lot of trust in him, and he had only known him for a few days. Well, sometimes it worked like that. You'd only just met someone and it was like you'd known him all your life. He folded the draft over and tucked it in his pocket with the list. June stepped forward with a bag and held it out toward him.

"I packed you some food for your trip," she said. "It ought to help a little."

Slocum took the bag in one hand and with his other doffed his hat.

"Thank you, ma'am," he said. "I surely do appreciate it."

It wasn't long before Slocum was on the trail again. He mused as he rode along. He had never thought that he'd be hauling a load of goods for a store. Especially with no pay for the job. He guessed that he liked those two as much as they seemed to like him and trust him. He couldn't think of another damn reason for sticking his nose into this business. Any other time, if he'd done something like this, he'd have called himself stupid. He'd have said that he ought to pack up and get out of town, just like he told Patton he was actually doing. Then he asked himself if he was really doing it for June, and he told himself no. That couldn't be the reason.

He wondered just why he had told ole Patton that he was leaving town. Was it something about the man? He wasn't sure why, but he did not trust Patton. Maybe he suspected Patton of being behind this trouble. If Patton was the guilty party, then he wouldn't be expecting Slocum to return in two weeks' time with a load of goods for Glover. The ole boy sure had a good-looking daughter, though. Slocum had to give him that.

He rode that day away with no incidents, stopping to eat along the way. The food that June had packed for him was sure good, too. It was about the best he had ever eaten along a trail. That night he made a small camp and slept well enough. In the morning, he woke up and cooked himself a breakfast of the food that June had prepared. He had three cups of coffee, smoked a cigar, broke camp and headed out.

He rode half the day without incident. He really anticipated no trouble. As far as anyone knew, he had left town to wander the trail aimlessly once again. No one knew that he was going for a load of goods for the Glovers. No one except the two Glovers and himself. Around noon he made another small camp and fixed himself a meal. He was about to finish up when he saw a rider approaching from the north. His Colt was on his hip. He was ready for whatever might happen. He sipped his coffee and waited.

The rider pulled up a few feet away. "Howdy," he said. Slocum responded. "Mind if I get down?"

"Help yourself," said Slocum. "You'll find a cup in the saddlebags yonder."

The man got down off his horse and walked over to where Slocum had indicated the saddlebags. He dug in one side and found a tin cup which he brought to Slocum's fire. He poured himself a cup of hot coffee.

"Much obliged," he said.

Slocum sipped at his coffee, but he kept a sharp eye on the stranger.

"That's a nice-looking horse you got there, mister," said the man. "It's what they call an Appaloosa, ain't it?"

"That's what they call it."

"I don't suppose you'd want to trade it."

"Nope."

"Some cash to boot?"

"He ain't for sale," Slocum said. "Even if he was, no one can ride him but me."

The stranger laughed. "I never seen a horse I couldn't ride," he said.

Slocum shrugged. "He still ain't for sale. You hungry, mister?"

"I sure could use some grub."

Slocum gestured toward the pan sitting beside the fire. "Help yourself," he said.

The man grabbed up the pan and ate voraciously. Slocum finished his coffee. He started gathering up his things, making ready to hit the trail again, but still he kept an eye on the stranger, who was still eyeballing his horse. When he had all his gear packed up, but not loaded onto his horse, Slocum pulled out his Colt and leveled it at the man.

"What's this?" the man asked.

"Take off your gunbelt and lay it aside," Slocum said. The man did as he was told. He looked at Slocum nervously. "I ain't got nothing to steal," he said. "All I got is my ole horse, and he ain't near as good as yours."

"You want to try my horse?" Slocum asked.

"What?"

"You think you can ride him?"

The man laughed nervously. "Yeah," he said. "I think so."

"Get on him then," said Slocum. "Ride him."

The man stood up slowly. He looked from Slocum to the Appaloosa and back again. "All right," he said. "I will."

"If you can stay on him," Slocum said, "we'll trade. But you only get one try. Fair enough?"

"Fair enough." The man walked slowly over to the side of the big Appaloosa. He gathered the reins. The horse nickered. The man took hold of the saddle horn. The horse stirred. The man got a foot in a stirrup and swung himself up into the saddle, and the horse bolted, nearly throwing the man off backwards. Then the horse stopped quick, turned and jumped. He kicked up his legs behind. Then he jumped high and twisted while he was in the air. The man flew off to the right, landing hard in the dirt. The Appaloosa stood still, looking at him.

Still holding his Colt on the man, Slocum walked over to the Appaloosa and tied the grub sack onto the saddle. Then he mounted up. He rode over to the side of the man's horse and took the rifle out of the scabbard, tossing it to the ground beside the man's gunbelt.

"Now get on your horse and ride," he said. "You can look over your shoulder now and then. When you can't see me no more, you can turn around and come back for your guns."

The man climbed into his own saddle, turned the horse and rode. Slocum sat still watching him. He saw the man turn and look back. He kept riding. Slocum let him get some distance away before he himself started riding. He looked back now and then to see that the man was still going south. At last, he kicked the Appaloosa in the sides, and the big horse leaped ahead. He did not think that the man would bother him anymore.

5

Slocum had more than half his ride to Denver behind him. He had met few travelers on the road. None to speak of. He'd had no trouble. He did not count as trouble the clumsy man who had showed interest in his horse. Even though he had planned this trip carefully, letting word out that he was leaving town, it still seemed all too easy. He told himself to stop worrying and enjoy the fact that his ruse had worked so well. Even so, he kept himself alert. There was no reason to get careless, just because things were going his way. It was about noon, and there was a town ahead. He decided to stop and rest and get a bite to eat. In a few more minutes, he reached the town. It was small, smaller even than Mesa Poquita, and there wasn't much there, but it was more than he needed.

Slocum took his horse by the stable for a good feed and a rubdown. He might as well have a decent break out of this stop, too. Then he walked down the street looking for a place to grab a meal. He spotted a place called Maude's Eats and headed for it. There were still a few people inside, even though it was past the lunch hour by the time Slocum went in. He sat down and ordered up a meal. While he was waiting, he noticed two cowhands giving him the once-over. He pretended not to notice, but he tried to recall if he had ever seen them before. He couldn't place either one of them. They were rough-looking hombres though, dirty and scruffy.

He did notice that the two ordered more coffee, and he got the idea that they were delaying their departure, likely because of him. They were waiting for him to leave. How come? he wondered. He also wondered if he was being paranoid—or just extra cautious. The waiter came over and brought his meal, and he set to, still keeping a watch on the two scurrilous bastards out of the corner of his eye. He finished his meal, and they were still sitting there drinking coffee. He had one more cup himself, then got up, paid and left the place. He made a point, on stepping out on the sidewalk, to check the horses at the hitchrail in front. In a boot on the right side of the saddle on a roan horse, he saw an old Starr .52-caliber rimfire carbine. Was it too much of a coincidence? How could those guys know about his trip to Denver for the Glovers? Or did they know? Did they just happen to be along the same trail? Were they even the right two guys? There could be two .52-caliber carbines in the area. It was possible.

He walked on, but he managed, as he was crossing the street, to look over his shoulder. The two men had come out of the eating place and were standing on the sidewalk looking in his direction. He made his way on down to the stable, paid the man and got his horse. As he mounted up to ride on, he noticed that the two horses were gone. So were the men. Maybe he was making too much out of this. Still, he would keep a sharp eye out along the trail. The man, or men, he was looking for were ambushing back-shooters, and he sure didn't want to take any unnecessary chances.

It was only a few miles out of town where Slocum found himself on a narrow trail with steep sides to his right and his left. He thought about the two men. They could easily have gotten out of town ahead of him while he was getting his horse. When he had mounted up, they had been nowhere to be seen. He stopped his horse and stared at the road ahead. It was only a short distance, but if two men were waiting in ambush, their victim would not have a chance. Slocum slid his Winchester out of its boot while he dismounted. He stood and looked around at the high rocks on both sides.

At last he spotted a likely way up to the top of the rocks, and he slapped the big horse on the ass. "Go on, boy," he said, and the Appaloosa trotted on ahead. Slocum scampered up the rocks and found himself a likely nest. He settled in and scanned the ridges ahead. He saw nothing. Where are the bastards? he thought. He had made up his mind somewhere along the way that the two men were waiting for him, that they were the same ones who had ambushed the wagon and killed the two men in it.

Then all of a sudden there was a loud shot, a .52-caliber shot, Slocum thought, and it was followed by the surprised nicker of a horse, almost for certain his Appaloosa. He hoped that the bastard had not hit his horse, and he looked for the place the shot had come from. He saw a movement, and he cranked a shell into the chamber of his Winchester and fired. All was still. He was sure he had not hit anyone. What he had done was prove to himself that the two bastards were after him, and he let them know that he was ready for them. He had spoiled their god damned ambush.

Now they would have to fight or flee, and he wondered where their horses might be stashed. There could be a way around back from the other end, but he doubted it. Their horses were likely down in the road ahead. There was no way he could see them because of the winding road with the high sides. He took the hat off his head and put it on the end of the barrel of his Winchester. Then, carefully peeking around the corner of a rock, he poked the hat up over the top. A shot rang out, and Slocum spotted the shooter. He lowered the rifle, repositioned it and fired. He heard a distant yelp.

They would not likely stick their heads up again. As quickly as he could, he scrambled down the side of the rocks to the road. Then, sticking to the same side the ambushers were on, he ran along close to the edge. When he had gone about the distance he imagined them to be, he slowed down to a walk, watching ahead closely. He moved a few more steps, and he saw his horse standing in the road. He inched forward a little more. There were the two horses he had seen in front of the eatery. There was no sign of the two men. Skulking bastards, he thought. He leaned back against the rocks to wait and watch.

In another minute, he heard the sound of footsteps coming down the rocks, slipping and scuffling. Then he heard muffled voices.

"Hurry it up, Orn."

"I'm going as fast as I can, damn it. I'm hurt."

Slocum tried to remember if he had chambered another round. He could not. He shifted the Winchester to his left hand and drew out his Colt with his right. They were right on top of him before he knew it, coming down the rocks just over his head. He heard a noise and looked up. There they were. He jumped out into the middle of the road, leveled his Colt and called out, "Hold it right there."

He had no choice in what happened next. One man went for his sidearm. The wounded man raised his Starr carbine. Slocum fired twice, fast. He didn't have the time not to kill. His first bullet hit the wounded man square in the sternum, knocking him back against the rocks. He slid down slowly, lodging between two boulders. Slocum's second shot angled up into the other man's heart. Blood spurted out freely. The man dropped his six-gun. His jaw dropped. His face went blank, and he pitched forward to land sprawling almost at Slocum's feet.

"Damn it," Slocum said. He had wanted to capture at least one of the men alive to question him. Now he had nothing but a Starr carbine and a name, Orn. It could be a first name or a last. He had no idea. He had two bodies, but he couldn't take them along. He still had to get on to Denver and get a wagon loaded to drive back to Mesa Poquita.

He holstered the Colt and walked over to his patient horse. Shoving the Winchester back into the boot, he led the Appaloosa over to the other two horses. Then he pulled the saddles off and tossed them behind some rocks. He did the same with the harness. Then he slapped the horses and sent them on their way. He shoved the two bodies behind some rocks. Keeping the Starr, he mounted up and rode on his way.

As he moved along, he tried to figure out how the two men had known he was on the way to Denver. He figured that they had to know he was making a run for Glover. If they had just thought he was riding out that way, leaving, they wouldn't have worried about him. There was no reason for them to ambush him unless it was to keep him from helping the Glovers. He couldn't imagine that either Larry or June had said anything, and he had not told another soul.

Now he was wishing that he had not agreed to make this trip. He was anxious to get back to Mesa Poquita and find out if anyone knew about someone called Orn who owned a .52-caliber carbine. Well, hell, it would just have to wait.

Back in Mesa Poquita, Pat Patton walked into Glover's Mercantile to buy some cigars. June was behind the counter. She greeted him, took his order, supplied it and collected the cash. He paid her.

"Thank you, Mr. Patton," she said.

"How are you two doing?" Patton asked.

"We're doing all right, thanks," she said.

"Well, I just worry about the two of you," Patton said. "I've been trying to figure out who could be behind these attacks on you. Has there been anything else?"

"No. Nothing since the night of the fire. I'm a little bit surprised by that."

"It's not surprising really," Patton said. "If someone's trying to ruin you, they probably think the job's been done. You're low on inventory. You've had a fire. You can't really last long now, can you?"

June puffed up. "We'll last all right, Mr. Patton," she said. "No one's going to run us out of business."

"I didn't mean to upset you," Patton said. "I was just being—Well, I'm sorry."

Just then, Larry walked in the front door. "Hello, Pat," he said.

"Hello, Larry. I was just leaving. I'm afraid that I've upset your wife. I'm sorry."

"What—"

"It's nothing, Larry. Mr. Patton. Really. I'm just a little touchy. That's all. Please forgive me."

"There's nothing to forgive. It was entirely my fault. Good day to both of you."

Patton walked out. Larry looked at his wife. "What was that all about?" he asked her.

"Oh, nothing, really, Larry," she said. "Pat just said something about us being through here, and I bristled up some. That's all."

"Well, it's about closing time, isn't it?" he said. "Let's lock up and go home."

On their way home, June told Larry exactly what it was that Patton had said. They chatted a little about it, then brushed it off.

"We've both got short fuses lately," Larry said.

"We'll have to watch it. Pat's really a nice man."

"Yeah. And he's been a good friend."

"And a good customer," said June. They both laughed.

They reached the house and went in. Larry closed and locked the door. Then he took his wife in his arms and kissed her, a long and lingering kiss. At last he backed off.

"Mmm," she said. "What brought that on?"

"We've let this business interfere with our lives for too long," he said. "I love you. How long has it been since I've said that?"

"Too long," she said. "I love you, too."

She took Larry by the arm and led him to the sofa in the living room. They sat down side by side and embraced, kissing again, their tongues probing each other's mouth. Larry began groping to get a hand underneath June's blouse. She broke away from the kiss and took his hand.

"Let's just get out of our clothes," she said. "Why waste time?"

Larry pulled off his boots, then stood up to strip. He was undressed before his wife, and he began helping her out of her things. Soon they stood naked facing each other. They stepped together in a warm embrace, feeling their bodies press together. June felt the cock rise from

Larry's crotch. She reached with both hands to hold it and play with it. Larry moaned with pleasure as he felt himself growing harder and stiffer, rising to meet the occasion.

"Sit down, darling," she said.

Larry sat, and June knelt before him. She looked up at him and smiled. His heart beat faster in anticipation. June stroked his cock. She leaned forward and kissed its head. It leaped in her hands. She licked it along the shaft, and Larry groaned out loud. She opened her lips and took the cock head into her mouth and slipped it out again. Then she moved in on it for real, taking in the entire length. She sucked it in slowly and pulled away again slowly, and then again, and again. At last, she bounced her head up and down, fucking him with her face. Larry humped and groaned.

"Oh, my God," he said. "Oh, June."

Feeling at last that she had produced a fine hard-on, she pulled away from it, stood up and straddled Larry with a knee on each side of him on the couch. She grasped his cock and guided it into her love hole as she lowered herself onto the throbbing shaft. Then she started rocking, sliding along his thighs. As his prick rammed in and out of her, Larry got even more excited. His two hands moved up to her tits and gripped them hard and kneaded, and his thumbs fondling her nipples and making them stand out.

"Oh, Larry," she said.

"Oh, June."

She stood up, turned around and sat down on him again, again grasping his cock with her hand and guiding it into her squishy tunnel of love. Larry reached around her with both hands to grasp her tits. June, with her feet planted firmly on the floor, began to bounce up and down furiously.

"Oh, oh, oh," she said.

"Fuck, fuck," said Larry.

Larry's panting grew faster and more desperate sounding, and June was afraid that he was about to come. She wasn't ready. She got off of him again and stretched herself out on the sofa on her back, crowding Larry off. He took the hint, stood up and turned, and as she spread her legs wide apart, revealing her wet and waiting pussy, he crawled between them, clutched his cock and aimed it at her hole. Falling forward, he missed the mark, but June grabbed his prick and shoved it in right where it was supposed to be. Larry gasped and thrust forward with all he had, driving himself completely inside her. She reached around him, grabbing each cheek of his ass and pulling him into her hard and even deeper. She held him like that for a moment, his rod throbbing inside her.

Then she started slowly to thrust her hips, and Larry responded. They moved ever so slowly at first, but soon they began to thrust faster and harder. In another moment their bodies were meeting with loud slapping sounds, and June was moaning loudly. Larry pounded harder and harder, but June at last slowed him and stopped him once more.

"Let me turn over," she said. "I want you to get behind me."

He stood up for a moment while she turned on her stomach, then rose to her knees. Larry moved in behind her. He took his cock in his hand and moved the head up and down her crotch until it slipped in the proper hole once more, and then he began thrusting with all his might. He felt the pressure building deep inside him. He thrust again and again.

"Oh, God, Larry, I'm coming," June shouted.

"Me, too," he said, and the jism shot forth in great gushes. He thrust with his tool again and again until he was at last spent. His softening cock slipped out of her wet pussy, and he fell back to a sitting position on the couch. June turned to sit beside him and nuzzled her head against his chest.

"Larry," she said.

"Hm?"

"Whatever happens from here on, let's not let them take our minds off the important things in life again."

"I promise you," he said.

"We can't let anyone make us forget what we have together."

"I'm the most fortunate man alive," he said. "No one can take that away from me."

"And I'm the luckiest woman. Whoever it is causing us all this trouble," she said, "we'll survive it. We'll get to the bottom of it, all right? And we'll be all right, Larry. We'll be all right."

"Yes," he said. "Of course we will."

He pulled her closer to him and kissed her again, and their hands started once more exploring one another's naked body. When Larry once more felt a stirring in his loins, and when once more, so soon after, his cock began to rise and swell, it surprised even him. June's hand reached down and felt it, swelling and throbbing. She gave it a tight squeeze.

"Larry," she said, her voice feigning great surprise, "what's this? Again? So soon?"

6

It was late in the evening when Slocum arrived in Denver, so there was nothing he could do till the next morning. He found the address all right, and it was near everything he needed, just like Glover had told him it would be. He put his horse in a stable, found himself a cheap room and then went out to eat. He had a good steak dinner and walked across the street to a fancy saloon. He walked up to the bar and ordered a himself a whiskey. He tossed down the first one and ordered a second. It was good, warm and soothing. He sipped on that second one. In another couple of minutes, a saloon girl stepped up by his side.

"Buy me a drink, cowboy?" she asked.

Slocum looked at her closely. She wasn't bad, and she was a young one, too. But he knew what she wanted, and Slocum was not in the habit of paying for it. At least he thought he knew what she wanted, but a good close look at her made him wonder. She seemed a bit uncertain, a little unsure of herself. Even so, he wasn't really interested. He had other things to worry about. But not till the morning. Hell, he thought, why not help the kid out a little?

"Sure," he said. "I'll buy you a drink. But that's all."

"What do you mean by that?" She was defensive. That wasn't right.

"Just what I said, little gal. I'll buy you a drink."

He made a motion to the bartender, who brought a bottle and another glass and poured a drink for the girl. Slocum paid for it. The girl took it up and sipped. Slocum watched her carefully. He noticed that she winced when she swallowed. She wasn't used to the stuff at all.

"What's your name, honey?" Slocum asked.

"Millie," she said. "Short for Millicent."

"Millicent's a pretty name."

"Thank you."

"How long you been in this line of work?" he asked her.

"What?"

"You heard me. How long?"

"I—Oh, hell, I just started," she said.

"Just—"

"Tonight."

"You mean you haven't—"

"No." Her voice quavered, and Slocum was afraid that she might cry. "I haven't. Not yet."

A dirty man walked up to the opposite side of the girl from Slocum, leaned heavily on the bar and took her by the arm. "Hey, girlie," he said, "let's you and me go upstairs."

"I—I'm sorry," she said. "This gentleman just bought me a drink."

"Well, if that's all the cheap son of a bitch is intending to do with you, you'd just as well come along with me. I got more in mind than a drink."

Millie looked at Slocum, and he thought that he could read a quiet desperation in her facial expression. She looked terribly vulnerable. Helpless. Hell, she didn't even look old enough to be in a place like this.

"She's busy, pard," he said, and it was only then that he looked up and saw the man. He recognized the character he had met on the trail, the one who had been so interested in his horse. "Run along."

"You," said the man.

"Don't start anything with me," Slocum said. "I might have to run you off again. Or worse."

"You caught me by surprise the last time, mister. I'm ready for you now."

Slocum stepped around behind Millie and gently brushed her aside, stepping between her and the newcomer. "I'm asking you nice," he said, "for now. Go on about your business. The lady's busy."

"She said you bought her a drink. That's all. I mean to buy more than that. Turn that drink up, little whore. Then you won't be occupied no more, and we can go have us some real fun."

Slocum's Colt was out and cocked in a flash, its barrel was touching the end of the man's nose. The bully's eyes opened wide. He stood still, trembling, and his hands moved slowly away from his sides, away from his gun.

"Don't. Don't do it," he said. "I—I ain't got a chance here. I don't want to fight you. Hell, I don't really want her anyhow. Just—Just let me go. Huh?"

"Then you just move right along."

"Yeah. Yeah, I will." He backed away a few steps, then turned to the bartender. "Give me a bottle," he said. He dug into his pocket and pulled out some cash, which he threw onto the bar. He took the bottle and a glass and hurried on over to a table at the far end of the room, where he sat down and hurriedly poured himself a drink. Slocum watched him for a few more seconds, then turned away. The man was a bully and a coward, not one to worry about, at least not in a room full of people. He was the kind who would shoot from hiding, maybe, a real chickenshit. Slocum dismissed the man from his mind.

"Millie," he said, "tell me if I'm wrong, or if I'm butting in where I shouldn't, but I don't think you want to be in this place."

"I don't," she said, "but I got no choice."

"Everyone's got a choice."

"You don't understand," she said. "I'm all alone. I got no family. I owe Melvin some money, and this is the way he said I could pay it back to him. I don't have anyplace else to go."

"Where you living?"

"Melvin gave me a room upstairs."

"And he's buying your meals?"

"Yeah."

"I'd be willing to bet that you'll never get him paid off. If you really don't want to be here, leave right now with me."

"What?"

"Once again, you heard me."

"Where will we go?"

"I'll take you back with me to a little place called Mesa Poquita. I know some people there. You can find a job. A decent job."

"You mean it?" she said, speaking in a whisper. Even so, Slocum could detect a note of hope in her small voice.

"Let's go," he said.

He took her by the arm and turned to leave the saloon, but a big man in a fancy suit stood up from a nearby table and stepped out in front of them, blocking their way.

"You can take her upstairs, mister, but not outside. It's a house rule."

"Last I heard, this was a free country."

"She works for me."

"And I bet you make up the house rules," Slocum said.

"That's right."

"Your name wouldn't be Melvin, would it?" Slocum asked.

"That's right. I own this place."

With no warning, Slocum swung his right fist as hard as he could, catching Melvin square on the jaw and dropping him to the floor like a sack of flour. He lay there stiff and still—out cold. Just then the man from the trail jumped up and pulled out his six-gun. Slocum saw him just in time to jump in front of Millie and draw his own Colt. The man's first bullet smashed the mirror behind the bar. His second ripped a gash in the bar and ricocheted up to smash a bottle on the back shelf. Slocum's one shot drilled the other man through the middle. The man fell back against the wall and slid down to the floor, leaving a smear of blood on the wall above him. Slocum looked around quickly. No one seemed to have any idea of coming to the defense of either man, so Slocum holstered his Colt, took Millie's arm again and walked out of the place.

At his room in the hotel, Slocum unlocked the door. Millie looked up at him with big eyes. "No strings, Millie," he said. "This room is for you for tonight. Get a good night's sleep. I'll call for you in the morning."

She went into the room, and Slocum locked the door from the outside, pocketing the key. Then he walked over to the stable to sleep in the stall with his Appaloosa. "Move over, big fella," he said. "It's just like out on the trail." Over in the hotel room, Millie lay awake on the bed staring at the ceiling and thinking about Slocum. She wondered what manner of man he was. She could hardly believe her good fortune. He had saved her from a life of sin and shame, and then he had left her alone in his hotel room. What did he want? Did he want anything from her? She didn't think so, but she figured he had to want something. She wasn't worried about it, though. She thought that she could give him anything he wanted. It had been wonderful the way he had dropped Melvin with one punch, and then that other man, that awful one she had almost had to—She hated to think about it. He had taken care of that one, too. She liked it that Slocum had killed the man. She felt like a princess who had just been rescued by a knight in shining armor, and at last she fell asleep, with that thought in her mind.

Early the next morning, Slocum wakened Millie with a rap on the door. In a short while, she went to answer it. "I can't open it," she said. "It's locked."

"I know," he said. "When you're ready, I'll open it."

When at last she let him in, he handed her a package. She looked at him with curiosity, and he just said, "Open it." She did and found a new suit of clothes. "I think they're the right size," he said. "I'll step back out into the hallway, and you can try them on."

He went back out and shut the door, and in a few minutes, she opened it, dressed in the new clothes. They were jeans and a shirt. They fit her nicely. She turned around for Slocum to get a good look from all sides, and

Slocum did get an eyeful. He thought that she looked much better than she had the night before. Her pert young breasts shoved out the shirt in front in just the right way, and her ass surely did fill up the jeans. He tried to take his mind off of what it was thinking.

"I thought they'd be better for traveling," Slocum said. "We can get you some more when we get to Mesa Poquita."

"They're just fine," she said.

"Come on," said Slocum.

"Hey," she said. "Why are you doing all this?"

"Millie," he said, "I got nothing against whores. Mostly they're pretty nice ole gals. I don't make much use of them myself. Never figured I needed to. What I don't like is someone like you being forced to that life. And I got no use for a son of a bitch like Melvin."

He led her to the stable, where he got his horse, and then they walked, leading the Appaloosa, down the street to another place of business. There Slocum signed for a wagon load of goods. It was loaded and waiting for him. The man got the horses hitched in a hurry, and Slocum tied his horse onto the back. Then he helped Millie up onto the seat, climbed up himself and took the reins. He released the brake, flicked the reins, and they started to roll. There was only one way to go, and it took them back past the saloon where Slocum had rescued Millie. Upstairs in a room, looking out the window as they drove past, was Melvin.

He watched through angry eyes as the wagon rolled along by his place of business, and he ground his teeth together. When the wagon had moved on out of sight, he tore himself away from the window and hurriedly finished getting himself dressed. Then he rushed out of the room and down the long hallway to the landing at the top of the stairs.

"Bart," he yelled. "Bart, get your ass up here."

Soon a big man came running up the stairs. He was dressed in a suit that looked a bit too small for him, and he was wearing a derby hat. "Yeah, Boss?" he said, puffing from his run.

"Round up three more of the men right away," Melvin said. "Make it Sonny, Gid and Hooley. Make sure they're all well armed. Then get your ass over to the stable and get us five good horses. Bring them out front. Hurry it up."

"Okay, Boss, but what's up?"

"Did you see what happened downstairs last night?"

"No, but I heard about it."

"I just saw the son of a bitch driving a wagon out of town, and he had Millie with him. We're going to kill him, and I'm going to teach her a lesson she'll never forget. Now get going."

As the wagon rolled along the road out of town, Millie thought everything was all right. It never occurred to her that Melvin would follow them out of Denver. She had been nervous as long as they were still in the city, but as soon as they were out—safely out, she thought—she relaxed. Her head was full of thoughts about where she was going and what was going to happen to her. She felt as if she were going on a long and wonderful adventure with her rescuer.

Slocum had no such feelings. He knew Melvin's type. He doubted that Melvin would just let it go. Likely he had other girls on the string the way he'd had Millie. If Millie got away clean, the others might get ideas. Melvin couldn't afford to have that happen. Slocum was hoping that he had gotten out of town without Melvin or any of his cronies seeing which way he was going, but he couldn't be sure. The only advantage he had was that if Melvin and some of his hired bullies were to come after them, he knew that they would be coming up behind. He wouldn't have to watch out for ambushers in the road up ahead.

He glanced over at Millie, wondering if he should warn her about the possibility of attack, but she looked so relieved and happy that he decided to let it wait. They might not show up at all, and if they did, well, that would be time enough for her to become aware of it. For now he'd let her enjoy her mood. He wished he could move along faster, but he knew that he couldn't. The team of horses had a heavy load to haul. It wouldn't pay to hurry them. In fact, he knew that he would have to stop frequently to rest the animals. He'd just have to keep himself alert to anything coming up from behind. That was all.

He remembered the spyglass in his saddlebags, and he decided that the first stop he made, he would have to get it out and keep it ready. It was early, but in spite of himself, he looked over his shoulder. There was no one in sight. He knew that if Melvin were to come along, he wouldn't be coming alone. He glanced at the girl beside him, sitting there so unconcerned, so comfortable. He wondered if he had done the right thing, endangering the Glovers' load of goods by going to the rescue of this young thing. Maybe he had made a mistake, but he couldn't bring himself to think of it that way. Millie had needed help, and he had come along at the right time. That was all there was to that. Then Millie broke the silence that had been between them.

"You just don't know what it's like," she said.

"What?" said Slocum.

"To be free all of a sudden. To be free from—well, from something like that."

7

Slocum hauled up the horses at the top of a rise and set the brake. "What are you doing?" Millie asked.

He lapped the lines around the brake handle and stood up stretching. "Just resting the horses," he said, but he really had something else in mind. He climbed down out of the wagon and walked around to his Appaloosa, digging into his saddlebags for the spyglass. From this high point, he had a good view of the road behind them. At first he saw nothing, no one coming up, but he kept watching. Then he saw the five riders coming hard. He was immediately suspicious. He kept watching until they were close enough for him to recognize features. He only knew one of them, but that was enough. It was Melvin all right. No doubt about it. He folded up the spyglass and put it away. Then he moved back to the wagon seat, loosed the lines and released the brake.

"What did you see?" Millie asked.

"It's that damn Melvin," he said. "And four more."

"He's coming after me?" she said.

"It looks that way."

"Oh, God. He'll kill me."

"Don't worry about it," said Slocum. "He won't get you. I'll see to that."

He whipped up the team and moved ahead. Millie twisted around on the seat to look behind them, but the five men were out of sight as the wagon moved down the other side of the hill. Slocum knew, though, that the riders would be closing the gap between them pretty fast. He hurried the team along as fast as he dared. He knew that he could not outrun Melvin and the others. He was looking for an advantage somewhere along the road. The road started to rise again up ahead, and Slocum noticed a crop of boulders to the right. He slowed the team for the climb, but also to take a better look. As he moved past the boulders, he saw that there was a wide place in the road behind them. He pulled the team off of the road and stopped the wagon. He set the brake and tied the lines. Millie looked nervously behind them.

Slocum grabbed her by the arm and pulled her off the wagon seat. "Come on," he said. He picked up his Winchester with his free hand and led Millie up into the boulders. He stopped where he had a good view of the road behind. Putting Millie safely behind a small boulder, he positioned himself for the coming encounter.

"Where are they?" Millie asked.

"Don't worry," he said. "They'll show up soon enough."

In another few minutes the riders topped the previous rise and started down the other side. Slocum let them get about halfway down before he fired a shot into the ground just ahead of them. They jerked out their sidearms and looked around frantically as they stopped their horses.

"What the hell?" said Bart.

"Hold it right there," Slocum called out.

"It's five against one," Melvin shouted. "Just send the bitch out, and we'll ride back to Denver and let you go on your way."

"I don't believe that," Slocum said. "Even if I did believe it, I wouldn't send Millie out. Now listen to my terms. Turn around and head back for town, and I'll let you go. Otherwise, Mr. Melvin, I'll drop you first."

Melvin knew that Slocum's first shot could have easily killed him. He considered his options. They were sitting ducks there in the road. Slocum was only one man, but what difference did it make if Melvin would be the first one killed? "Come on, boys," he said. "Let's go back to town." He turned his horse, and the other four men followed. They started riding back toward Denver. From his perch up in the boulders, Slocum watched them.

"They're going back," said Millie excitedly.

"Don't count on it," said Slocum.

Soon the riders disappeared once more. Slocum tried to figure out what their next move would be. Maybe they would think that he had fallen for their trick and would just drive out again. If that was the case, they would simply wait a few minutes and try again. They might try to find a way around to the backside and slip up on him. He wasn't about to drive off, not with those five bastards out on the road after his hide, so he had to think about that second possibility. He did not think there was any way for them to ride around behind him. They would have to leave their mounts and climb the rocks. He had to have a better position to be ready for that. He looked around for a minute. Then he stood up. "Come on," he said to Millie.

He started to climb again. "Where are we going?" Millie asked him.

"I think they'll try to come up behind us," he said. "We have to get higher up."

In another few minutes, they reached the top of the outcropping of boulders. Slocum looked around but saw no one. He wondered if he had figured the bastards wrong. Then he saw a movement in the boulders. He cranked a shell into the chamber of his Winchester, pulled Millie down behind a boulder and ducked down himself. He watched carefully, and then he saw the head and shoulders of Gid. He waited. Gid moved some more, exposing more of himself, and Slocum raised his Winchester to his shoulder, took quick aim and fired. Gid yelped, straightened up and fell. Slocum looked around. He saw no one else.

"One down," he said. "Four to go."

Millie was trembling from fright, but she stopped short of crying. Slocum glanced over at her. He reached over and patted her hand, but he said nothing. There was nothing to be said. He watched the boulders to the north, waiting for another movement. The silence was thick. Then he heard scraping sounds, the noise made by boots slip-

ping on rock. He tried to locate the sound and looked in
that direction. At last he saw the figure of Hooley stand
up and look around. He fired again, dropping Hooley, but
just as he did, the other three popped up and began firing.
The bullets pinged off the boulder Slocum was hiding
behind. They were close, too close. He couldn't raise his
head to fire back. Millie pressed herself hard against the
boulder, wincing with each shot.

Slocum waited. They couldn't keep firing that way for-
ever. They would have to stop to reload. He waited it out.
When the shooting stopped, he looked up, ready to fire,
but the three men had all ducked down to reload. Slocum
grabbed Millie again and moved the two of them to another location. When the attackers popped up again, they
would have to try to find him. Maybe that would give him
time for a shot or two. He crouched down behind another
boulder and peeped around the corner. In another minute,
the three shooters raised up to fire. Slocum snapped off a
shot, and Bart dropped his weapon and grabbed for a
bloody left shoulder. Then he dropped out of sight. Slocum's second shot hit Sonny in the head.

The odds were much better now. There were only two
left, and one of them was wounded. He glanced over at
Millie and nodded. They moved to another hiding place.
Slocum looked out again, but the two remaining shooters
were still hidden. He waited for a while, but they did not
reappear. Finally, he concluded they were at a standoff.
He decided to make a bold move, and he took Millie again
by the hand and started back down to the road. Reaching
the bottom, he pushed Millie behind a boulder and
stepped out to stand beside the wagon. He looked up the
way they had come.

Suddenly Melvin appeared above, standing up in full
view. He held a revolver in his right hand. "God damn
you," he shouted, and he started firing. Slocum was pressing his luck, but Melvin had a difficult range for a revolver. He was foolish. His shots kicked up dust around
Slocum. Calmly, Slocum raised his Winchester and fired.
His shot was low. It tore into Melvin's left foot. Melvin
growled with pain and flinched, and as he did so, he lost

his footing. As he toppled off the boulder, he screamed. He bounced off a boulder not far below, and his screaming stopped, but he continued to fall, bouncing off boulders two more times before his limp body lodged in a crevice. Slocum could tell that he was dead.

That left only one man, and he was hurt. Slocum wondered if the man would give it up. His boss was dead. There really was no reason for him to continue, and he ought to head back for medical help if he had any good sense. Slocum waited. Then he heard the unmistakable sound of someone coming down the side.

He stepped over to the wagon and put down his Winchester. He watched, and in another minute the noises ceased. He stood waiting. Then Bart stepped out into the road. His left arm hung useless at his side, blood pouring down from the shoulder wound.

"It's all over," Slocum said. "Melvin's dead. Ride back and get some attention paid to that shoulder."

"I ain't going to do that," Bart said. "You hit me, and I don't ride away from that."

"I wish you would," said Slocum. "You and me got no fight."

"We do now," Bart said. "Go for your gun."

"After you," said Slocum.

Bart suddenly reached for his revolver with his right hand, but Slocum was faster. His Colt barked, and Bart dropped, his own gun unfired. He had a new hole in him. This one was in his chest. He crumpled in a heap in the road. Millie stepped out into the road and stared at Bart's bloody and unmoving body in disbelief. Slocum walked over to stand beside her. He put an arm around her shoulder and held her close. She was still trembling.

"It's all over now," he said.

"Melvin?" she said.

Slocum pointed to a spot up on the side of the outcropping where Melvin's body was lodged. She looked and saw it there. "I can't believe it," she said. "I'm really free."

Slocum nodded. "You're free," he said. "Let's get going." They climbed back up on the wagon box, and Slo-

cum started to drive away. He got them well away from
the site of the fight and the dead bodies, and then he
looked for a place to stop. The sun had reached a spot
almost overhead. Slocum pulled off the road at a wide
spot, and led the horses to a nearby stream. Then he built
a small fire to cook some lunch. Coffee was ready before
the food, and he poured two cups, handing one to Millie.
She took it gratefully and sipped. Then she looked up over
the cup at Slocum and smiled.

"You're really something," she said. "Just yesterday I
was—"

"Forget about that," Slocum said, interrupting her. "It's
all over."

"Yes. Thanks to you."

"I'm just glad I happened along," he said.

"God," she said. "You came along just at the right time.
I can't hardly believe it."

Slocum dished out their meals on two tin plates and
handed one to Millie.

"Thank you," she said. She took a bite. "This is really
good. You're a good cook, too," she said.

"When a man spends a lot of time out on the trail
alone," Slocum said, "he has to learn to cook. Otherwise
he goes hungry."

They finished the meal and drank some more coffee.
Slocum got the horses ready and cleaned up the campsite.
Then they climbed into the wagon once more and hit the
road. Millie was considerably more relaxed. She began to
talk about one thing after another. Slocum was beginning
to feel fatherly. She was quite a bit younger than he was,
and he had just rescued her from a life of—well, from a
life that was not of her own choosing. When she moved
over closer to him, it made him nervous. Then she scooted
again. This time she was touching his side. He shot a
sideways glance and saw that she was looking up at him
smiling. He became very uncomfortable.

This was a new feeling for Slocum, to have a beautiful
young woman coming on to him and making him uneasy.
He wondered why he had developed this fatherly feeling
for her. He wished that he had not. But there was nothing

he could do about it. It was there, and he was stuck with it. But what was worse, he had several nights of camping along the road ahead of him yet before they would reach Mesa Poquita. Those nights could be rough. He figured that he was as honorable as the next man, but he did have his limits.

He glanced at her again, and this time she snuggled even closer, took hold of his arm with both her hands and squeezed it tight. Oh, God, he thought, they would indeed be rough nights. There was no doubt about it.

When they stopped to camp that night, Slocum made himself as busy as he could, tending the horses and then fixing up the camp. He made the beds up a good distance from one another, with the fire in between them. Then he cooked their meal and made some more coffee. He cleaned up the dishes. At last, there was nothing more to be done. He could no longer put things off by pretending to be busy.

"You'd better get some sleep," he said. "We have a long day ahead of us tomorrow."

"Are you going to bed?"

"No. I think I'd better keep a watch for a while," he said.

"But you killed Melvin and those men."

"There could be others," he said. "The last time Glover had a wagonload headed into Mesa Poquita, the driver and guard were murdered and the wagon was wrecked. It could happen again. I have to stay alert. You go on to sleep now."

She looked disappointed and reluctant, but she only said, "Good night," and began to get ready. Slocum moved quickly away from the light of the campfire. He found himself a spot against a tree in the darkness and sat down to watch. He really didn't think that he had anything to watch for, although there had been that incident with Orn and the other fellow. He did have that .52-caliber rifle. It could be that someone else back in Mesa Poquita knew about this trip. Even if that were so, though, he hardly thought that whoever was behind the attacks on the Glovers would have sent out more than the two men.

He sat up for some time thinking about these and other things, and at last he dropped off to sleep. When he woke up the following morning, he built up the fire and fixed some breakfast and coffee. He was nervous while they ate. Then he broke camp and hitched the horses. Millie walked over to him. She had to grab hold of him, because he was moving fast, trying to keep himself out of her grasp.

"Do we have to be in such a hurry?" she said.

"We have a long trip ahead of us," he said.

He got the wagon going again, and again she sat too close for comfort. Something was going to have to give, he thought. He was going to have to have a serious talk with her and tell her how he actually felt about her. He was going to have to get her to back off. Either that or, he was going to have to—Well, after all, he was only human.

8

As the days went by, Slocum began to feel the strain of
his incredibly unusual stance toward Millie. He found
himself struggling inside. When she did not sit so close
to him on the wagon seat, he found that, in a strange way,
he missed the closeness. And at night, he discovered himself moving away to his watch position more and more
reluctantly. He found himself looking at Millie with lust-
ful eyes. She was a beauty. There was no getting around
that. And she had made it more than obvious that she
wanted him, that she wanted to give herself to him. What
the hell, he said to himself. After all, she had been a
whore before he rescued her, a reluctant one, but a whore
still. What would it hurt? Still, he resisted. He resisted for
as long as his body would stand for the resistance.

But at last he caved in. He just couldn't take it any
longer. He told himself that he had been acting the fool.
Here was a beautiful young woman throwing herself at
him, and he was holding himself aloof, acting like he was
too good for her or like he was afraid of her. True, he
was old enough to be her father, but he was behaving as
if he were as young as she, even younger. As the wagon
rolled along one evening, he suddenly reached out to put
an arm around her and pull her close to him. Her heart
raced. She could scarcely believe what was happening. At
last. He was giving in.

"I think we'll stop a little early tonight," he said. "If that's all right with you."

"Of course it's all right," she said. She smiled up at him. "I am a little tired of the road."

Slocum pulled off at the next likely campsite. He felt an almost desperate throbbing in his loins, but he had put this off for so long that he didn't want to rush things. He took care of the horses, and then he laid out the camp. This time, though, he did not roll out the beds on opposite sides of the fire. Then he prepared their meal, and they ate. He felt like he couldn't get through with the meal fast enough, and he felt foolish for having such thoughts. It would be far from his first time. What the hell was wrong with him?

Slocum had been only pretending about the dangers of the road. He did not really believe them to be in any immediate danger. He had taken care of the two men who attacked the wagon on the way up to Denver, and he had finished off Melvin and his nefarious crew. The trip back to Mesa Poquita from this point on should be a relatively peaceful one. He had pretended danger as an excuse to sit up at night away from Millie. But unknown to Slocum another danger lurked behind them. It was the man who had shown such interest in the Appaloosa, and later in the saloon in Denver had taken a shine to Millie. Slocum had had two chances to kill the man, and he had let him go the first time, believing him to be a coward and a bully. The second time, he had shot the man but not bothered to see if he had killed him. The man bore a grudge. He was following them on the road.

The man topped a rise in the road and came to a sudden stop. Slocum had called a halt to the day's travels a little early. The man could see the camp a ways down the road. He did not want to ride in on Slocum in the daylight, even though it was already fading. Slocum was much too dangerous for that. The man had pushed his luck twice with Slocum and so far he had been lucky, but he had a feeling that one more time could easily be his end. He had been hurt bad, and he really shouldn't have been out on the trail again so soon. But he was mad. When he met up with Slocum again, he meant for it to be a surprise. He meant to shoot Slocum in the back or while he was sleeping. He would get him this time. This time would be the last.

He eased his horse off the side of the road and pulled off the saddle, wincing with pain. He made himself a small camp, but he built no fire. He did not want to do anything that might alert Slocum to his presence. He drank water and ate cold, hard biscuits, cursing Slocum the whole time. When he had eaten all he could stomach, he checked his weapons, a .36 Cooper revolver and a Marlin .45–70 rifle. Both were clean and loaded. He wanted to be ready when he found his chance, so he chambered a shell in the Marlin. Then he carefully leaned it against a tree trunk and sat down to smoke.

Mars Cooper, for that was the man's name, had been following Slocum almost since he drove out of Denver. Melvin and his gang had interfered, and Mars had hung back watching. His feelings had been mixed during the encounter between Melvin and Slocum, for he had nothing but hatred for Slocum, yet he wanted to exact his own revenge. Had Melvin won the fight, Slocum would be dead. That would not have been ideal, but it would have been all right. What would not have been all right was that Melvin would have had the woman back. And he would have had the Appaloosa. Cooper wanted them both for himself. His plan now was to kill Slocum in a sneaky and cowardly fashion and then take Millie and the horse for himself. He had not thought about how long he would hold on to Millie. Sooner or later, he would have to kill her, too. He knew that. That was all right. He'd have his fun first.

He smoked his cigarette, rolled another and smoked that one. The wound in his belly hurt him, and the smoke made him cough. When the coughing fit passed, he cursed. The sun was low in the sky. Then he stood up and moved out into the road. He looked down at the camp again. Smoke was rising from the fire, and he fancied that he could smell the coffee even from this distance. He wanted to kill Slocum all of a sudden just for a cup of that fresh coffee. He could see the wagon clearly, but the camp itself was in the trees. He could not see the fire; nor could he see either Slocum or the woman. He had been watching them ever since they started the journey, and he knew that Slocum made their beds separate from each other and that Slocum sat up at night keeping watch. He would have to be careful. This time, his moves had to be all just right—no slipups, no mistakes.

Down in the camp, Slocum cleaned up after the meal. Millie helped him this time, smiling the whole time in anticipation. Darkness was closing in on them. The main light was from the campfire. Slocum added a few sticks to the fire, figuring that it would be a while before it got any more tending. He straightened up and turned to see Millie sitting on her bedroll looking at him with a sweet smile on her lovely face. She had already removed her boots, and while he stood there watching, she began to pull her shirt off over her head. Slocum felt the stirring again. This time it was much more urgent. Millie tossed aside her shirt, revealing a pair of bounteous young breasts. Slocum longed to grasp them and to suck on the nipples. He moved toward her.

Out on the road, Mars Cooper had moved in much closer. He had a better view of the camp. He could see the fire, but he could not clearly see the figures. He thought that he could see the woman sitting on her bedroll, and he knew that Slocum's roll was always across the fire from hers. He also knew that Slocum sat up at night keeping watch. He had to find Slocum. He moved in closer, slowly, trying to stay as quiet as he could. His gut hurt. He felt beads of sweat pop out on his forehead, and his hands were slippery wet on the Marlin. Then he saw a movement.

It was Slocum, standing up, moving toward the woman. They must be talking. He hadn't yet taken up his watch post. Cooper raised the Marlin to his shoulder and took careful aim. His shot should hit Slocum right between the shoulder blades. The line of fire was good, too, safely away from the woman. He squeezed the trigger, and the shot shattered the night air, silencing the singing bugs and the night birds that had been calling.

Slocum had just dropped to one knee, moving toward Millie, his rod beginning to stand up in anticipation, when the shot sounded. He heard the bullet whiz over his head. Quickly he moved to Millie and pulled her away from the fire. "Stay here," he said. He had already taken off his gunbelt and laid it aside. It was a few feet away on the ground. His Winchester was in the wagon. "Damn," he said.

"Who is it?" said Millie.

"God damned if I know," said Slocum, scrambling for his Colt. He grabbed it up and moved into shadows away from the fire and under the trees, away from Millie, for he did not want to draw any fire in her direction.

Out on the road, Cooper had run for cover as soon as he realized that his shot had missed the mark. He was trembling for fear, and he was angry at himself for missing such a shot, for losing such a chance. If only he had fired an instant earlier. He hunkered behind a boulder on the far side of the road. "Damn, damn, damn," he said, as he cranked another round into the Marlin's chamber. "God damn. I'm into it now." He knew that he could not get up and run. That would expose him on the open road, even in the darkness. Besides, the wound in his belly hurt him too much if he tried to run. He had no choice. He had to hunker down and fight it out. He was glad, at least, that he had the Marlin. He could fight Slocum at a distance. He watched the campsite with shifty and frightened eyes.

Slocum, on the other hand, knew that he could not simply remain still. There was a man out there on the road who had tried to kill him with a rifle. He couldn't just sit there. He had no idea where the man was located. He was just out there on the road. He had a rifle, and Slocum had only his Colt revolver. He would have to find the man, and he would have to get close enough for the Colt. Either that or make his way to the wagon to get his rifle. He thought about the lovely young body that had been waiting so anxiously for him. "Damn that son of a bitch," he said.

Slowly he moved over to another tree, a bit closer to the road. There was no shot. Perhaps his movement had not been detected. He moved again. In three more moves, he was at the edge of the trees. The wagon was parked a short distance away in the open. He could try for it, but he would be vulnerable for a few steps to a shot from up on the road. He had to do something, though. He knew that. There was nothing to do but expose himself. Draw a shot from the bastard. That way he might be able to tell where the man was hiding.

He had to be careful, though. There was more at stake here than just his own life. He wasn't too worried about his life. He had risked that over and again for much more trivial reasons. But he had the goods for the Glovers. The existence of the store depended on his bringing them on in to Mesa Poquita. And then there was Millie. There was no telling what would happen to Millie if he were to get himself killed out here on the lonesome road. Who the hell was that son of a bitch? he wondered.

Cooper was getting more nervous by the minute, crouched there behind his boulder. He wondered what Slocum's next move would be. There had been no shot returned from the camp. He began to think that maybe he had hit Slocum after all. Maybe Slocum was lying down there dead. Maybe he wasn't dead, only wounded. A man like Slocum could be dangerous even when he was wounded. Cooper wondered all of a sudden if he had chambered a shell. He couldn't remember. Slowly and carefully he cranked the lever of the Henry to be sure. Yes. He had chambered a shell. He realized then that he had taken his eyes off the camp for a moment. He looked back quickly.

Just as he did, Slocum ran from behind a tree down below. Cooper raised his rifle fast, too fast, and fired a shot. In the dim light, Cooper could see dust kicked up behind Slocum's feet. Quickly, he chambered another round, but by the time he had the Henry back up to his shoulder, Slocum had grabbed the Winchester out of the wagon and run to another tree. Cooper fired anyway, and he felt foolish for wasting another shot. He could no longer see Slocum. He cranked the Henry one more time. Suddenly he was very much afraid, more afraid now than mad. The wound Slocum had given him before was hurting terribly.

Slocum was behind a tree on the far side of the clearing, where the wagon was parked. He filled the chamber of the Winchester and squinted toward the road. He had seen a flash when the man fired, but he had been running, so he couldn't be sure just where it had come from. He had the man located in a general area. He thought that he was on the far side of the road. There were a number of small boulders lining the road along there, and he could be behind any one of them. Slocum knew that his Winchester was carrying a full load, and so he came up with a plan. He picked a range of boulders along the road. He was pretty sure the man was behind one of them. Starting on the left, he fired at a boulder. The bullet spanged off of the rock. Then he shot the next one and the next. With his fourth shot, he heard a yelp and some movement. It was not a yelp of pain. It was a yelp of fright. At least, Slocum thought so. He stopped sweeping and fired two more shots at that same boulder.

Cooper was hunkered down as low as he could get, pressing himself against the boulder and clutching his Henry rifle close to his chest. He was whimpering and flinching at each shot. He knew that Slocum had located him, and he was beginning to think that he had made a big mistake in trying to get the son of a bitch so soon after having been shot. At last the shots stopped. Slocum had just been wasting ammunition, and he knew it. Cooper tried to think of what he should do. He knew which tree Slocum was hiding behind, unless Slocum had moved again while Cooper had been snugged down. He peeked out from the boulder. No shot came. The darkness was now his ally. He set his eyes on the tree he believed Slocum to be behind.

He raised the Henry to his shoulder again, terrified of

exposing himself, moving very slowly and praying that the darkness was covering him. He took aim at the tree and waited. But the waiting was terrible. At last he fired. A shot was returned, and Cooper felt shards of rock pepper his face. He huddled down once more.

Slocum had the man now. He knew exactly where he was hiding. All he had to do was wait the man out. He could not think of any other way. It would be stupid to go charging. He couldn't get a shot at the man unless the fool exposed himself. He had just tried a foolish shot. Maybe he would do so again. But maybe this time he would have more patience. Maybe the only way for Slocum to get a shot at him would be for Slocum to expose himself and draw the man out. He decided to do that.

He stepped around the tree and raised his Winchester, and when he did, the man popped up and took aim. Slocum fired first. The man screamed and fell back. Slocum stood still beside the tree. He had no idea whether his shot had killed the man or only scratched him. He didn't want to find out by being stupid. He stayed at the side of the tree watching the boulder for any sign of movement, listening for any sign of life.

Behind the boulder, Cooper was clutching a shattered shoulder. He knew that he was done for now, and the knowledge made him bold for the first time in his life. If he had to die, he thought, he might as well take Slocum with him. He slipped the Cooper revolver out of his belt and smiled. He had always thought that it was very appropriate for him to carry a Cooper. It had his own name. He drew back the hammer and laid the revolver on his belly. The wound there was bleeding again.

"Slocum," he called out. His voice was weak.

Slocum figured that the man was hit bad. "What do you want?"

"Slocum, I'm done for."

"You brought it on yourself. Who the hell are you?"

"Never mind about that. I could sure use a smoke before I die. Roll me a smoke and bring it on up here to me. I ain't got much time."

"Toss your rifle out," said Slocum.

"Here it comes." Slocum watched as the Henry flew out from behind the boulder to land in the road. He started walking toward where the man waited. He held his Colt ready just in case. Close to the boulder, standing in the road, he stopped. "You still back there?" he said.

"I'm here," said Cooper. "Come on. Give me a smoke before I die."

Slocum took a couple of steps, then moved to the other side of the boulder. He stepped in closer, and then he saw Cooper. Cooper was expecting him to show on the opposite side. He tried to whirl and fire, but the pain from the two wounds slowed him down, and Slocum fired first. His bullet killed the man. He walked over to take a good look and to be sure, and then he recognized the man.

"I'll be a son of a bitch," he said. "I thought I'd already killed you."

He turned slowly to walk back toward the camp. Millie would be waiting.

9

"Hell, it's more dangerous along this damn road than I thought," Slocum said to Millie. "We can't afford to relax. At least, I can't. Go on now and get some sleep."

Millie sighed, obviously disappointed, but she had been frightened by the sudden attack from Cooper, and she did not argue. She went on to bed. Slocum, again, posted himself beside a tree. He tried to imagine who else could come along, and no one came to his mind. But then, there had been the attack by the man with the .52-caliber rifle. That was obviously the work of whoever it was trying to break the Glovers. That scoundrel was bound to know by now that his attempt had failed. The man might try again. And he could try with anyone at just any old time. Any stranger could be hired to do his dirty work.

Slocum decided that his vigilance need not be a pretense. It should be real. He also decided that his attitude toward Millie had been correct in the first place. The sudden and unexpected appearance of Cooper was proof enough of that in Slocum's mind. He had almost given in to his baser instincts, and Cooper had come along to interfere. It just wasn't meant to be. He was almost ashamed of himself for even considering crawling into the sack with the young girl. But, damn, she had been trying hard to get him. And she was not an easy one to resist. For some reason, he thought again of June Glover, and he wondered if he would be able to resist June in a similar situation.

The rest of the ride back to Mesa Poquita was uncomfortable and uneventful. There were no more attacks, but Slocum remained on alert, and the girl sat aside, mostly silent and almost huffy. Slocum could not think of a trip he had been on in his entire life which he was so glad to have come to an end at last. They drove into Mesa Poquita around noon on a Sunday. Slocum knew it was a Sunday only when he saw the people leaving the church. He slowed the wagon across the street from the church and waited. In a couple of minutes, the Glovers came out. When they saw him, they hurried across the street to greet him.

"Slocum," said Glover. "You made good time."

"We're so glad to see you," said June. "Did you have any trouble?"

Slocum reached down beneath the seat and hefted the big rifle out, handing it to Glover. "Ran into this feller," he said. "He won't bother you no more. And, uh, I found this little gal in Denver. She was in some trouble, so I brought her along. You know that salary you once offered me? I kinda figgered you might want to hire her on. I'll stay just for my room and board. Her name's Millie."

"Well, sure," said Glover. "We can give it a try."

June reached a hand out toward Millie. "I'm June Glover," she said. "This is my husband, Larry. We're pleased to meet you."

"Well, I'll drive the wagon on over to the store," Slocum said.

"We'll be right along," Glover said.

A little later, at the store, Slocum and Glover unloaded the wagon, and Millie helped June inventory and put things away. When they were at last done, Glover locked the store again, and the four of them went to the café for a late lunch. They had coffee all the way around, and they were waiting for their meals.

"So, Millie," said June, "do you think you'll like it at the store?"

"I'm sure I will," Millie said.

"Good."

"Has there been any more trouble?" Slocum asked.

"Now that you mention it," said Glover, giving his wife

a look, "there was a stranger came into the store a few days ago. He bought some stuff and then started in to complaining. I offered to give him back his money, but that didn't work. He said I had the only place around where he could buy what he wanted. He wound up punching me in the face. I was about to get it on with him, but Elgie came in just then and stopped it. The guy took his stuff and left."

"That was it?" Slocum asked.

"Yeah. But I got to thinking about it later, and I believe he came in just to start a fight."

"Well, there's some men like that," Slocum said, "but with what all's been going on, I'm inclined to believe it's all connected. Is the man still around town?"

"I haven't seen him again," Glover said.

"Hmm." Slocum stroked his chin.

"Maybe it wasn't related to the other stuff at all," Glover said.

"Maybe," Slocum said, but he did not sound convinced.

Their meal was served, they ate, and then they walked back to the store. Slocum went into his room in the back and packed up all his belongings. It did not take much time. Everything fit into his blanket roll and saddlebags. As he came walking out into the store, Glover looked surprised. "What are you doing?" he said.

"Millie's going to need a place to stay," said Slocum. "I figured I could move out of here and let her have the room. If that's all right with you."

"Well, sure," said Glover, "but—"

"Where will you go?" said June.

"I'll just make me a camp," Slocum said. "I've done it aplenty."

"I don't want to put you out," Millie said.

"Don't worry about it. Aw, hell, I'll get me a room at the hotel."

Just then the door opened, and a big, burly man in a red checkered shirt stepped inside, not bothering to shut the door behind himself. Slocum noticed Glover stiffen, and June set her jaw.

"We're not open," June said. "It's Sunday."

"Well, you're here," the man said. "It won't hurt you none to sell me some tobacco."

"Sorry," said Glover. "Like she said, we're not open."

"Just get me some tobacco," the man said, walking on over to the counter.

"Your money's no good here," Glover said. "Get out."

"You can't do that. You got the only store in town."

"You should have thought of that before you punched me out."

"I could do it again."

"Is this the man?" asked Slocum.

"He's the one."

Slocum stepped over in front of the man. "You got a name?" he asked.

"You got one?"

"I'm Slocum."

"Well, I'm Bull Cutter. What of it? All I want is some tobacco."

Slocum moved behind the counter and got a bag of tobacco. Bull reached for it, but Slocum held on. "Pay for it first," he said.

Bull reached again, but Slocum gripped it hard. Bull swung a big first, catching Slocum on the jaw and knocking him back against the shelves. Slocum tossed down the bag of tobacco and rubbed his jaw. He started to walk around the counter. Bull backed up and doubled his fists.

"Come on, tough guy," he said.

"It's what you come in here for," Slocum said. "Let's step outside."

"What's the matter? Afraid something might get broke?"

Bull swung again. This time, Slocum sidestepped and drove a right into Bull's gut. Bull winced and stepped back, but he was unhurt by the hard right. Slocum quickly shot a straight left into Bull's face. Then he swung a right at Bull's jaw, but Bull managed to block that one. He drove his own right into the side of Slocum's head, staggering Slocum back. Then he shoved a row of shelves over. Glover made a move toward Bull, but Slocum stopped him.

"Stay out of this, Larry," he said. Then he whipped out

his Colt and cocked it all in one motion, leveling the barrel at Bull's gut. Bull stopped still. "I ain't armed," he said.

"Like I said," Slocum growled, "let's go outside."

Bull backed out the door, and Slocum followed. Glover and the two women moved out right behind him. With Bull standing out in the street, Slocum handed the Colt to Glover. Then he walked toward Bull.

Bull grinned. "All right, tough guy," he said. "I'll take you apart."

He swung a roundhouse right, but Slocum ducked under it, stepped around to the left and drove a fist into Bull's kidney. Bull groaned and swung wildly. Slocum backed away. A small crowd began to form to watch the action. Bull moved in toward Slocum, and Slocum jabbed him on the nose with a left and followed with a right cross to the side of the head. Bull howled and charged, throwing both arms around Slocum's shoulders. The force of his charge drove both men to the ground. Bull's weight falling on top of Slocum knocked most of the wind out of Slocum's lungs. He struggled to get Bull off him, but he was weak. He sucked hard, trying to get some air back into his lungs.

Bull sat up on Slocum's chest, his hands around Slocum's throat. Slocum tried to pry loose the fingers, but it was no use. He knew that he wouldn't last much longer. The world around him was growing dimmer by the second. He squiggled around until one of his legs was between Bull's legs, and he sharply raised a knee, smashing it into Bull's balls. Bull roared in pain, loosened his grip on Slocum's throat and rolled over onto his back, his knees drawn up to his belly. Slocum rolled over and got himself up to his hands and knees. Slowly he managed to draw some air into his lungs. He stood up, staggering some.

At last Bull struggled to his feet, straightening himself up slowly. He doubled his fists in front of his face and glared at Slocum. Slocum stepped in quickly, driving two hard fists into Bull's middle. Bull doubled over, and Slocum hit him on the right side of the head, then on the left side. Bull tried to cover his face with his arms. Slocum pounded a fist down between Bull's shoulders, knocking him to the ground.

"Get up," he said. "Come on."

He grabbed hold of Bull's shirt and dragged him to his feet. Bull was sagging.

"You only came round to wreck the place, didn't you?"

Bull did not answer, and Slocum smacked him again.

"Who paid you to wreck the store?"

Slocum felt a hand on his shoulder, and he dropped Bull and whirled to defend himself. Just in time, he saw that the hand belonged to Elgie Fletcher, the sheriff. "Hold on right there," Fletcher said.

"Sheriff, this son of a bitch came in determined to wreck the store. I was about to get him to tell who hired him."

"That ain't the way to do it, Slocum," Elgie said. "Let it go."

"Damn it, Fletcher—"

"I said let it go, Slocum."

Slocum let Bull go, and Bull dropped to his knees. Slowly he got back up and staggered over to the nearest watering trough to duck his head.

"Shit," said Slocum.

"Now what was that all about?" Fletcher asked.

Glover stepped forward. "That man came in the store," he said. "I told him we were closed. He demanded service and took a punch at Slocum. Slocum made him bring the fight out here."

"That's all?"

"Yeah."

"Except that he was in the store once before," said June, "and he struck my husband."

"All right," said Fletcher. "I'll take it from here." He walked over to where Bull was still washing his face. "Come on along with me," he said.

"What for?" Bull muttered.

"Don't give me no trouble," said the sheriff. Bull started walking and the sheriff moved along with him. They were headed for the jail. Slocum walked to the watering trough and splashed some water on his face. A young man stepped through the small crowd and moved toward the Glovers.

"Oh, hi, Thad," said Larry Glover.

"Howdy, Mr. Glover. Say, what was all that about?"

"It's a long story, Thad," Glover said. "It seems like someone's trying to run us out of business."

"Really?"

"I'm afraid so," said June.

"It all started with that wagon wreck."

"Maybe sooner, now that I think about it," June said. "There were some small things. I didn't think too much about them at the time."

"Yeah," said Glover. "She's probably right. Anyhow, there was the wagon and the two killings. Then the fire in the store. Slocum went after supplies for us, and he was attacked on the road. Then this guy came in and started a fight. He broke up the store a little inside. Slocum stopped him."

Slocum was walking back over to the store from the trough about then, and Thad gestured toward him. "This Slocum?" he asked.

"Yeah. Slocum, I want you to meet Thad Slater. Sam Slater's his father. He owns the ranch out—"

"Oh, yeah," said Slocum. "Glad to meet you."

"Likewise," said Thad. "I was just hearing about how you been helping the Glovers. I'm glad you're here."

"Yeah," Slocum said.

"Well, we're sure glad," said June. Standing nearby, Millie cleared her throat. "Oh, Thad. This is Millie. She's going to be working with us."

"Glad to meet you, Mr. Slater," Millie said.

Thad took off his hat and held it in front of his chest. "It's Thad, miss," he said. "Mr. Slater's my old man. Oh, and uh, the pleasure's all mine."

Slocum took note of Millie's smile. He had mixed feelings. He guessed that this Thad was a good-looking enough chap, but till he figured out this mess, everyone was under suspicion. And, after all, the ambush spot Slocum had located had been on the Slater ranch. He told himself that he would have to have a talk with Millie the first chance he got.

10

"Miss, Millie," said Thad. "Did they say that you're working here in the store?"

"I haven't really started yet," Millie said, "but, yes, they very kindly offered me a job here. Thanks to—Mr. Slocum."

"Well, I'm very glad of that, and I'll have to thank Mr. Slocum, too."

Millie's smile broadened, and Slocum's mixed feelings grew a little more muddled. Thad had certainly taken Millie's thoughts away from Slocum. For that, he should be grateful. But he still wasn't sure about Thad's possible involvement in the troubles that the Glovers had been having. If Thad was guilty, Slocum did not want Millie to get involved with him. That's all the crooks would need, someone on the inside of Glover's establishment to feed them information. Not that Slocum suspected Millie would do such a thing consciously, but if she had fallen for some guy, she might spill something without thinking about it. It was a hell of a problem. Of course, he told himself, he could be jumping the gun. Nothing had really happened yet between the two.

"Miss Millie," said Thad.

"You can drop the 'Miss,' " Millie said, "if you don't mind."

"All right then," said Thad. "Millie, I hope you won't think I'm being too bold, but there's a dance Friday night.

I'd sure be proud to take you. It will be a good time for you to get acquainted with folks around here."

"Thank you, Thad," Millie said. "I'd be pleased."

Thad beamed. "That's great," he said. "I'll pick you up—Where?"

"Right here," Millie said. "I'll be staying in the back room of the store."

"All right then. I'll be here about seven o'clock—with a buckboard."

"I'll be ready," said Millie.

Thad excused himself then, put on his hat and walked to where his horse was tied. He headed out of town, toward the Slater ranch. Slocum ambled over to Millie's side. "Millie," he said, "I don't mean to interfere, but I wish you'd be careful."

"What do you mean?"

"You just got to town. You don't know anyone yet. The Glovers have been having trouble for some time, and anyone could be behind it."

"What are you trying to say? Are you suspicious of Thad?"

"I'm suspicious of everyone," Slocum said. "Till I find out who's behind it all."

"Well, there's no harm in going to a dance, is there?"

"No, Millie. I just said to be careful. That's all."

Slocum moved his things out of the back room, and Millie moved in that night. The Glovers went home for the night, and Slocum had a couple of drinks in the saloon. He was about to ride out of town to locate a good campsite, even though he had told the Glovers that he would get a room, when he had a troubling thought. He recalled the night he had been sleeping in the store and the two men had come in to burn the place down. He decided that it wouldn't be safe to leave Millie there alone. He decided to keep watch. He found a chair on the main sidewalk and moved it into deep shadow. Then he sat down to watch.

He smoked a cigar, and then he just watched. It was somewhere past midnight when he caught himself about to doze off. He stood up to stretch his legs. Suddenly he stopped and moved back into the shadows again. There were two men moving sneakily toward the Glovers' store. Slocum stood still and watched them for a while. They stopped and looked up and down the street. Then the one in the lead moved to the front door. As the man started to try to jimmy the door, Slocum pulled his Colt and ran toward them.

"Hold it," he shouted.

The two jerked their heads around quickly to see the threat. One man pulled a gun, and Slocum fired. He didn't have time for a careful aim, and his bullet smashed into the man's left arm right at the elbow. The man screamed and dropped his gun. Slocum was on the two by then. He turned his attention quickly to the one as yet unhurt, but the wounded man quickly reached down with his left hand and picked up his fallen gun. He smacked Slocum hard on the head. As Slocum dropped to the sidewalk, the wounded man said, "Let's get the hell out of here." The two ran as fast as they could.

Slocum moaned and rolled over on the sidewalk. He reached up with his right hand to rub his sore head. Slowly his thought processes began to work again, and he got himself up to his hands and knees. Feeling around for his Colt, he found it and grasped it. Then he got himself up to his feet, but he staggered back against the wall. He stood there for another moment allowing his head to clear. Then he looked up and down the street, but the two had disappeared. "Damn it," he said. He knew that he had hit the one, and he knew that he had hit him in the arm. The man wouldn't be hard to spot unless he went into a hole somewhere to wait it out. Likely he would do just that. "Damn it," he said again, wishing he had gotten a better look at them. He cursed himself too for having nearly dozed off. If he had been alert, he would have had a better chance of catching them.

Slocum woke Millie in the morning and took her with him to the eating place for breakfast. He looked around for the Glovers, but they were not there. He figured they must be having breakfast at home. He did see Patton and his daughter and spoke to them as he and Millie moved on to a vacant table. They got some coffee and placed their order. While they awaited the food, Slocum debated with himself whether or not to tell Millie about the attack he had thwarted the night before. He didn't really want to frighten her, but he had warned her about being too loose with her new acquaintances. Maybe he should let her in on it. He was about to tell her when the breakfasts arrived. They ate in near silence. When they were done at last, they had some more coffee. Slocum made up his mind.

"Millie," he said, "I'll talk to Larry when he gets to the store here in a while. I want you to move over to the hotel."

"Why?" she said. "It's a nice room."

"I told you what's been going on here," he said. He looked around to make sure that no one was in hearing distance, and he kept his voice low. "I stayed awake last night watching the store. Two men tried to break in. I stopped them, but they got away. I think you'll be safer in the hotel."

A worried look came over Millie's face, and she said, "God, Slocum, what did they want?"

"Hell," he said, "how do I know? Likely they just meant to wreck the store again. They've killed two men, though. There's no telling what they might do."

"But what could happen to me?"

"You'll be safe enough staying in the hotel," he said, "and they won't pull anything in the daylight when the store's open."

She sat silent for a moment sipping her coffee. Then she looked up at him again. "Slocum?" she said.

"Yeah?"

"You think that Thad has something to do with all of this?"

"I don't think anything, Millie. Like I said before, I'm suspicious of anyone and everyone till I find out. The men who were killed were shot from ambush from a spot out on the Slater ranch."

"Oh, God."

"That don't mean that Slater or his son had anything to do with it. I rode up there without anyone knowing about it, and anyone else could have done the same thing. I just want you to be careful. That's all. And I want you to move out of that room. Okay?"

"Okay," she said. "Slocum? I just thought you were jealous. I thought you didn't want me to have any fun unless—"

"Don't worry about it, Millie. I don't blame you for thinking that. Let's get on over to the store now."

They got up to leave, and Slocum paid the bill on the way out. Walking over to the store, Millie said, "John, I hope I haven't been acting too much the fool."

"Oh, no, Millie," he said. "You're just new in town, and I brought you into a kind of a dangerous situation, but don't you worry. You'll be all right."

They got to the store just as the Glovers arrived, and Larry unlocked the door. They moved on inside.

"Good morning," said June. "Come over here with me, Millie, and I'll show you what's what."

Millie followed June around the counter, and Slocum stepped over close to Larry. "They tried again last night," he said.

"What happened?"

"Two men started to try to break into the store. I shot one of them. Then I turned on the other one, and the one I shot whopped me over the head. They got away, but they didn't get to do whatever it was they come to do. I wish I'd got a good look at them, or at least brought one of them down."

"Well, at least you stopped them," said Glover. "Damn. I wish I could think who might be behind all this. How's your head?"

"Aw, it's all right. Keep your eyes open, though, for a fella with a hurt right wing."

"That where you shot him?"

"Yeah."

"Say, uh, let's go have a cup of coffee. What do you say?"

"Sure."

They walked right back over to where Slocum had already had his breakfast and ordered them each a cup of coffee. When they felt alone enough, they resumed their conversation.

"What do you think our next move should be, Slocum?" Glover asked.

"I can't think of a damn thing," said Slocum, "except wait for their next move."

"It's making me crazy. June seems to be doing all right, but it worries me. I'm afraid she'll fall apart all at once."

"Likely June's tougher than you give her credit for being," Slocum said. "You just watch yourself. Take it easy. It'll all come out in the wash soon enough. In the meantime, I recommend you move Millie into a hotel room. I'll move back into the store. After last night, I'd feel better about it. I should've suggested that in the first place. I guess I just wasn't thinking clear."

"Yeah, sure. I'll take care of that today. You can move back in tonight."

"That'll be fine," Slocum said. "I don't know how soon they'll dare try anything again at the store, but I sure do want to be ready when it happens the next time."

"Yeah. Say, it seems to me like we're no closer than we ever were."

"The only thing we had to go on was that fifty-two-caliber carbine, and that's no good now," said Slocum.

Glover lifted his coffee cup and took a sip.

"You know," said Slocum, "there might be something we could do."

"Tell me."

"Put out the word that you're sending me off for a special order. You don't have to say what it is or who ordered it. Just that you're sending me off for it. Someone's bound to try to stop me."

"That sounds like it could be dangerous," said Glover.

"It could be," said Slocum. "Let's try it anyway."

"Okay, but you'll have to try to keep from killing them this time."

"I'll do my damndest," said Slocum. "And try to keep myself from getting killed at the same time."

"Say, the big dance out to Slater's is tomorrow night," Glover said. "You want to wait till the next morning before you start out?"

"Might as well," Slocum agreed. "That'll give us time to get the word around anyhow. There's no sense in making the trip unless our man knows about it."

Slocum stood up, and when he next spoke, he raised his voice some. "Well, let's head back over to the store, Larry," he said. "I've got a lot to do to get ready for that trip."

They walked back and found Millie dealing with her first customer. She sold some cloth to a lady from town. Taking the lady's money and giving her change, Millie said, "Thank you, ma'am. Come back again."

"I will, young lady," said the woman. She turned to face June. "I think you've got some good help there, Mrs. Glover. She's a nice addition."

"Thank you," June said. She turned and smiled at Millie as the woman left the store. Larry and Slocum were also smiling at Millie.

"Going to work out just fine, it seems," Slocum said.

"I think so," said Millie, beaming.

"I know so," said June.

Patton walked into the store just then.

"Hello, Mr. Patton," said June. "Have you met our new clerk, Millie?"

"It's a pleasure," said Patton, removing his hat.

"How do you do, Mr. Patton," Millie said.

"Millie, would you like to take care of Mr. Patton?"

"Surely, Mrs. Glover. Mr. Patton, how may I help you?"

"Well, now," Patton said, "you might say that you'll allow me to take you to the dance tomorrow night."

Millie blushed. "I'm sorry, Mr. Patton. I've already promised someone else."

"What a pity. May I know who?"

"Mr. Slater," Millie said.

"Old Slater?"

Glover laughed. "No, she means young Thad," he told Patton.

"Oh. Well." Patton shrugged. "Maybe another time."

"Perhaps," Millie said. "Now what can I help you with today?"

"I had a rowdy bunch in the saloon last night," Patton said. "I need to replace some glasses. Do you know—"

"Right over here, Mr. Patton," Millie said, and she led him across the room.

"She's going to be just fine," Slocum said to Glover.

"I think so," Glover said.

"Don't forget to get her that room at the hotel."

"Oh, yeah," said Glover. "I think I'll run over and take care of that right now."

11

Millie got herself all ready for the big dance and hurried back over to the store from her hotel room. She had not seen Thad Slater again to tell him of her move. When she arrived at the store, she found Slocum sitting out front on the sidewalk casually smoking a cigar. "Oh, hello, Slocum," she said, a little embarrassed. She recalled the admonition Slocum had given her about being careful with her new acquaintances.

"Howdy, Millie," Slocum said. "You're sure looking pretty tonight."

"Thank you," she said. "Slocum?"

"Yeah?"

"Don't worry about me. I'll watch out for myself. I promise."

Slocum looked down the street to see Thad Slater driving a buggy into town. He nodded in that direction, and Millie looked.

"Are you going to be at the dance?" she asked.

"I might look in on it a little later," Slocum said. "I'd kind of like to meet old man Slater."

Thad hauled up in front of the store and climbed down out of the buggy to give Millie a hand up. He nodded at Slocum.

"Have a good time," Slocum said.

"Thanks," said Thad. "I'm sure we will." He moved around the buggy to crawl back into the seat. Giving a snap of the reins, he started the rig moving again, turned it around in the street and headed back in the direction from which he had come. Slocum puffed on his cigar and watched them go. He rolled over in his head his plans for the night. Earlier he had tried to make up his mind whether he should go to the dance or stay at the store. It occurred to him that this would be a good night for whoever it was to hit the store again. Most everyone would be at the dance. He did want a chance to meet old Sam Slater to see what he thought of the man. At last he had decided that he would go out to the dance and meet Slater, stick around for a little while and then go back to watch the store. He figured that if they did hit the store again, they would wait till late. He finished his cigar and walked down to the livery stable to get his horse.

As he rode out toward Slater's ranch, he considered again the reason for the attacks on the store. There wasn't any reason that anyone could come up with. No one else seemed to be interested in wanting to run the store or any other store. The attack on the wagon, the first one, had come from Slater's ranch, but anyone could have slipped up there. Patton had offered to buy the store, but it seemed as if he had only done that to help out the Glovers. He had also offered to loan them money. Slocum had heard him make that offer. Both men were, according to Larry Glover, good customers. On top of all that, everyone seemed to like the Glovers. It just didn't make any sense.

The dance was in full swing when Slocum arrived at the ranch. It was out in front of the big barn, and in the doorway of the barn, a few men with fiddles and guitars were sawing and plunking away. A number of couples were dancing around the yard. A long table was laid out with food and drink, and there were plenty of folks, male and female alike, lined up at the table. Slocum dismounted and tied up his big Appaloosa. He stood for a moment surveying the scene, and then he walked toward the long table. A big man with a handlebar mustache, wearing a suit, excused himself from a conversation and walked to meet him. Extending his hand, the big man smiled and said, "Howdy, stranger. I'm Sam Slater."

Slocum took the offered hand. "John Slocum," he said. "Pleased to meet you. Looks like you have a big time going on here."

"Yeah," Slater said through his broad grin. "I think everyone here's having a fine old time. There's plenty of food and drink on the table there. Help yourself."

"Thanks," Slocum said. "I will."

He walked toward the table, and Slater walked alongside him and kept talking. "I know everyone else here," he said. "Have you been around long?"

"Not long," said Slocum. "I'm working for Larry and June Glover."

"Oh, yeah. I heard they'd hired a helper."

"Actually two helpers," Slocum said. "A girl named Millie to work in the store. Me, I'm going out for another load of goods in the morning. It's a special order, I guess. I don't really know. All I do is drive the wagon."

"I don't get into town very often," said Slater, "but I heard that Glover lost a driver and a guard not long ago. True?"

"Yeah. That's right." Slocum reached the table and forked a big chunk of beef. "I guess I'll have to keep a careful lookout."

"I'd say so."

"Say," said Slocum, "do you mind if I ask you a question?"

"Ask away."

"I met a couple of fellows a while back. They had the look of cowhands. I don't recall the one fellow's name, but one of them went by the name of Orn. One of them carried a Starr fifty-two-caliber carbine."

"Yeah?"

"Do you happen to know them?"

"They used to work for me," Slater said. "They didn't show up for work one morning. I been wondering what happened to them. Where did you run across them?"

"Oh, I just run into them out on the road," said Slocum. "I don't think you need to be expecting them back."

Slater opened his mouth as if to speak but thought better of it. He changed directions. "I hope things are going along all right for the Glovers," he said. "I'd hate for anything to happen that would cause them to—Well, I'd just hate to see it happen."

Slocum nodded toward the dancers. Larry and June were among them. "You can ask them how things are going," he said. "They're right over there."

"I will," said Slater. "Right now, I'm asking you, though. How does it look to you?"

"We're getting along okay," Slocum said. He walked past the beer barrel to where some whiskey bottles sat on the table. Getting a glass, he poured himself some and took a sip. "You have good taste in whiskey," he said. "Thanks."

"You're welcome," Slater said. "Enjoy yourself." He turned and walked away. Slocum tried to figure out what to make of the man, but he couldn't really tell anything from their brief conversation. Maybe, he told himself, he'd been too abrupt with the old fellow. He'd just have to wait and see. He had learned one thing, though. The murderers had worked for Slater. Slater had readily admitted it. Of course, Slocum had not said they were the murderers. But Slater had acted ignorant of what had become of them. Even if they had been working for him— that is, if they had been attacking the Glovers for him— he would act ignorant, of course. So there were two strikes against Slater: the ambush spot and the murderers.

But the killers could have been working as cowhands for Slater and doing dirty work for someone else at the same time. And if they were cowboys for Slater, they would have known the ranch well enough to have set up the ambush. Slocum did not feel much closer to a resolution of the problem. He had a couple of facts, but by themselves, they didn't really mean much of anything, much less prove anything.

He walked over to the dance area and dodged several couples in order to tap Thad Slater on the shoulder. "Mind if I cut in?" he said. Young Slater shrugged and stepped back, and Slocum took Millie in his arms and started to dance with her. "Having a good time?" he asked her.

"Wonderful," Millie said. "Thad's a real nice gentleman. And so is his father."

"Yeah," said Slocum. "I met the old man."

"And?"

"I just met him. That's all."

"But do you think—"

'I don't think anything, Millie. Not yet. Do me a favor, though. Keep your ears open. You hear or see anything that might help me, let me know about it. Okay?"

"Sure," she said.

Slocum felt a tap on his shoulder and looked back to see Thad. He turned Millie back over to the young man. "Thanks," he said. He walked back toward the long table, but before he reached it, he found his way blocked by Patricia Patton, the saloon owner's daughter. He reached up and touched the brim of his hat.

"How do you do, Miss Patton?" he said.

"I don't have a dancing partner," she said, with a coquettish look on her face.

"Well, let's go," said Slocum, taking her by the hand. He moved back out into the dancing area and started to move to the music, his right arm sliding around her tiny waist. She was looking up at him and smiling. Slocum glanced around and saw her father standing between the dance area and the long table—watching.

"You seem distracted," Patricia said.

"I'm trying to read the look on your daddy's face."

She laughed. "Don't worry about him. He doesn't care what I do—or who I do it with."

"That sounds like some kind of an invitation," Slocum said.

"Take it how you like." They danced awhile. Then she spoke again. "It was."

"What?"

"An invitation. You interested?"

"I sure could be."

"Let's get out of here," she said.

"Just like that?"

"Why not?"

"Your daddy, for one reason."

"I told you, he doesn't care what I do—"

"Or who you do it with. Yeah. You said that. But I'd just as soon he not see us leave here together."

"Oh, all right."

"I'm staying at the Glovers' store," Slocum said. "If you're serious, if you could find your way over there a little later—"

"I can."

"I'll see you there then," he said. "Thanks for the dance."

He walked her back out of the dance area and tipped his hat. Walking past Patton, he said, "Howdy, Mr. Patton."

"How do, Mr. Slocum."

He noticed that the Glovers had stepped out and were sitting this one out, so he went over to see them.

"I'm going back to the store," he said. "You two just relax. Have a good evening. I'll keep an eye on things."

"Slocum," said Glover, "you don't have to—"

"I know," Slocum said. "I'll see you in the morning."

Slocum headed for his horse. He had to pass by old Slater on the way.

"Leaving so soon?" Slater said.

"I have things to do. Thanks for the hospitality."

He mounted up and headed back toward town. The ride back was a lonely one. Slocum put his horse away for the night and walked to the store. Everything seemed all right. If anyone was planning to hit the place, it would be later in the night, just like he'd figured it. He wondered if he had been wise to invite Patricia Patton over. She had asked for it, and he had not had whatever it takes to turn her down. Ever since he had almost caved in with Millie, he had been—well, he just hadn't had what it takes. And then there were his troubling feelings regarding Larry Glover's wife. Hell, he thought, maybe Patricia wouldn't show up at all. Maybe the spoilers wouldn't show up either. Maybe it would just be one of those nights.

He went to the back room of the store and found a bottle. Then he went out to the store and sat in a chair in a dark corner. He uncorked the bottle and took a sip of

the good whiskey. He'd have to go slow. He'd already
had a drink out at Slater's place. In case anything happened at the store this night, he couldn't afford to be
drunk, not even a little bit. He could sip a bit, though,
before it would bother him or slow him down any. He
knew his limits well enough. He watched the street
through the front window. It was like a ghost town out
there. He saw one lone cowboy ride down the street and
disappear. He took another sip of whiskey, replaced the
cork and set the bottle on the floor beside his chair. Then
he dozed off.

He woke up with a start when he heard the sound of
someone unlocking the front door, and his Colt was out
in a flash. He watched as a figure moved into the store in
the darkness. He was about to thumb back the hammer
when he recognized Larry Glover. He relaxed with a
heavy sigh and stood up, holstering the Colt.

"I'm over here, Larry," he said.

"Oh, Slocum," said Glover. "Everything all right here?"

"Everything's just fine," said Slocum. "I thought I told
you and June to relax and have a good evening."

"Hell, Slocum, we did. It's getting late. We're on our
way home, and I just thought I'd stop by and check on
you—and the place."

"Oh. I guess I slept longer than I thought. Anyhow,
you go on ahead and take June home. I'll be all right
here."

"Okay," Glover said. As Glover walked out the door,
Slocum followed him. June was sitting in the buggy in
the street. Slocum tipped his hat.

"Good night, Mrs. Glover," he said. "Sleep well. I've
got everything covered."

"Good night, Slocum," June said. "And thank you."

Slocum stood on the sidewalk watching as the Glovers
drove away. He had turned to go back inside when he
saw a shadow down the street. Someone was moving toward him cautiously, staying in shadow. He waited. The
figure came closer. If it was someone up to no good, Slocum thought, the sight of him standing out front on guard
might send them away. Trying to act as if he had not seen

anything, he yawned and stretched and turned around to go back inside. He shut the door behind himself and latched it. It was dark inside the store. No lights were burning. Whoever was outside would not see him standing there by the window. He waited, and at last the solitary figure moved into his view. It was Patricia.

12

Slocum unlatched the door and opened it, and Patricia started with surprise. She saw Slocum and put a hand over her left breast and took a deep breath. "Oh, you scared me," she said.

"I didn't mean to," Slocum said. "Come in." Patricia stepped inside, and Slocum closed and latched the door again. She stepped in close to him and put her hands on his shoulders. "You took your time," he said.

"The dance was so much fun, I just couldn't leave," she said. "I must have danced with every man there, at least once. Then I came home with Daddy, and then I had to sneak out of the house after that."

"I thought he didn't care what you do," he said. He leaned forward to kiss her, and it was a deep and passionate kiss, not hardly just a hello. "Or who you do it with."

"Well," she said, panting, "there is such a thing as propriety."

"Well now," he said.

"You forgive me?" she said.

"What for?"

She smiled and looked deep into his eyes as her body wriggled closer and tighter against his. They kissed again, long and lingering. Slocum broke away at last and took Patricia by an arm. He started leading the way to the back room. "Come on," he said. They moved slowly across the storeroom, Patricia hanging on to Slocum's arm tightly. When they reached the door to the back room, Slocum opened it and stood aside for her to go in first. She stepped in. He followed. Slocum motioned toward the bed. She gave him a look.

"Aren't you going to close the door?" she asked.

Slocum had already thought of that. As anxious as he was to plow this lovely field, he did not want to be shut off from any action that might take place outside. At the same time, he did not want to tell her why he was leaving the door opened.

"The front door's latched," he said. "No one'll be around."

"But I—"

He pulled her to him and kissed her mouth to shut it up. Then he undid her dress with the practiced hands of an expert. She slithered out of it and let it fall to the floor. Then she stepped back and sat down on the edge of the bed. Slocum slipped his shirt off over his head and tossed it aside. Then he watched as she pulled off another piece of clothing, and then she watched as he did. Soon they were both naked, she sitting on the bed and he standing before her. Her eyes looked down to where his manhood stood erect and ready.

"Oh my," she said. She leaned back until she was lying on the bed, and as she scooted over to make room for Slocum to join her there, she allowed her legs to open up, spread wide apart. Slocum moved in and crawled between them. He lowered himself until his weight was pressing down on her, and his lips found hers once again. Her arms went around him and held him tight, crushing her own body with his. He moved around, trying to find her wet hole with his stiff rod, but he was not having much luck with the search. Patricia giggled and loosed her arms from around his back, moving between the two of them, reaching down with her hands to fondle his rod and his heavy balls. At last she took the head of his prick and guided it to the opening of her pleasure tunnel. Once he knew he was there, Slocum thrust down. He slid easily into the cavern, gliding smoothly all the way in, and as he did, she arched her back, throwing her pelvis upward, making sure that she had the entire length deep inside her.

"Ahhh," she gasped.

Slocum put a hand on each of her lovely rising tits and squeezed, and then he started to pump with his pelvis.

"Oh," she said with each thrust. "Oh. Oh. Oh."

Across the street, two rugged-looking cowhands lurked in the dark shadows between two buildings. One sucked on the stub of a roll-your-own cigarette. The other was watching the front of the store.

"It looks okay to me," the watcher said.

The smoker took the butt out of his mouth and blew smoke. "Anyone on the street?" he asked.

"The whole damn town looks deserted to me."

"The store?"

"It's dark. Hell, the gal's already gone to sleep."

The smoker took one last drag and flipped the remains of the cigarette aside. "Well," he said, "let's go do it."

Both men hitched at their gunbelts and started to cross the street. They glanced up and down the street as they crossed, not because they were afraid of getting run down, but lest anyone should appear on the street to get a look at them.

In the back room, Slocum pumped himself empty into Patricia's depths. He lay still on top of her, breathing deeply. "That was wonderful," she said.

"I'm just getting warmed up," Slocum said. He shifted his weight, and as he did, his head turned just the right direction to get a look at the front door through the open passageway into the back room. He saw the silhouettes of two figures, looking for all the world as if they were about to break in. "Hey," he said, rolling quickly off of Patricia and off of the bed and running for his Colt.

Patricia looked up and saw the men. She jumped out of bed and ran naked to Slocum's side. As he raised the Colt for a shot, she grabbed his arm. He fired, but his shot went low, crashing into the wooden door a couple of feet up from the floor.

"Yipe."

They heard one of the men outside squeal. Then they heard a voice.

"I thought you said the girl was staying back there."

"That's what Thad said."

"Well, let's get out of here. She might shoot higher next time."

Slocum shook Patricia loose and ran for the front door. He unlatched it and threw it open, stepping out onto the walk in his birthday suit and looking down the street just in time to see the two men disappear around a corner. He was sure that one of them had been limping. They were gone, though, and he lowered the Colt. Patricia came up beside him.

"They got away," he said.

"I've got to go home," she said, and she turned and walked toward the back room. Slocum stood another moment on the sidewalk. Then he stepped back inside, closed and latched the door. He followed Patricia to the back room where he found her pulling on petticoats.

"What'd you spoil my aim for?" he asked her.

"What?"

"You grabbed my arm just as I shot. How come?"

"Did I? I . . . I don't know. I was frightened, I guess. That was very upsetting, as I'm sure you can imagine."

He sat down on the edge of the bed and watched her finish dressing. Then he got up and helped her fasten her dress. She turned to walk away, but Slocum stopped her.

"I'll get dressed and walk you home," he said.

"That won't be necessary," she said. "I can find my way."

Slocum was reaching for his trousers. "Yeah," he said, "but—"

Patricia was at the front door by then. She unlatched it and hurried on out, leaving the door standing open. Slocum dropped his trousers back to the floor and walked to the front door. He stepped out and looked after her for a moment. Then he shut the door and latched it. He returned to the back room and sat down again. He was thinking about Patricia. She had certainly spoiled his aim. But had she done it deliberately? It might have been as she said. She might have just been frightened and grabbed for him. He wondered. And what had the one man said after Slocum's shot? The girl was supposed to be sleeping in the back room. Millie? It had to be. And then the other had added, "That's what Thad said." Thad Slater.

Thad Slater, son of Sam Slater, owner of the ranch from where the deadly bullets had been fired that started all the trouble. The ranch where the cowboy with the Starr carbine and his partner had once worked. All of a sudden, everything was pointing at the Slaters. Thad had picked Millie up at the store. Perhaps she had not told him about her move to the hotel. He had told those two that Millie would be staying in the store, in the back room. They would have thought it would be a pushover to break into the place.

But then, Slater had made no move toward the store in the open, and Patton had offered to buy it more than once. What would the saloon owner want with the store? And why had Patricia spoiled Slocum's aim?

Slocum managed at last to sleep, and in the morning, he was up early, dressed and over to the eating place for his breakfast. Along the way, he found a trail of drops of blood. He was drinking his first cup of coffee when Patton and his daughter came in. They spoke to him as they walked by his table. Patricia gave no hint with a look or a sound of what had happened the night before. They sat at a table across the room. Slocum finished his coffee and had a refill as the Glovers came in. They walked over to his table.

"May we join you?" June said.

Slocum stood up and said, "Please do."

They all three sat down. Glover waved a greeting to Patton, and it was acknowledged. The waiter came over and brought two fresh cups of coffee. He took the Glovers' order and left again. In another minute, Sheriff Elgie Fletcher came walking in. He strode over to their table and spoke to the Glovers and Slocum.

"Good morning, Elgie," June said.

"Slocum," said Fletcher, "you still staying in the back room over to the store?"

"Yeah."

"Anything happen over there last night?"

"Nothing, Sheriff," said Slocum. "Why do you ask?"

"Aw, it's likely not important, but the way things has been, I thought I oughta check. Someone heard a shot late last night."

"No," said Slocum. "Nothing."

The sheriff touched the brim of his hat and went over to another table. In a couple of minutes, Pearly came in and joined him. He nodded at the Glovers and at Slocum as he walked by, a surly nod, Slocum thought.

They finished their breakfasts and went to open the store. Slocum waited for a chance to get Larry alone. Then he spoke in a low voice. "I didn't want to alarm June," he said. He told Glover what had happened in the store overnight. "I think I hit the one," he said. "In the leg or in the foot. I could see him limping, and I found a blood trail on my way over to the eating place this morning."

"Let's take a look," said Glover. The two men walked to the front door. Slocum pulled it open, just as June stepped out. "Oh," said Larry, "we'll be right back."

They stepped out and shut the door. Glover looked down. "Over to the right," said Slocum, and Glover turned his head. Sure enough, he spotted a splotch on the sidewalk. He looked around some more. "Walk along," said Slocum, stepping down into the street. They took a couple of steps, and Slocum said, "Right there." Glover spotted a second splotch. They followed the splotches across the street and between two buildings. The trail ended behind the bank.

"It looks to me like they had a couple of horses tied up here," Slocum said.

"Can we track them?"

"I'll try," said Slocum. "First, do you think I ought to tell ole Fletcher?"

"Well, I—"

"I didn't say nothing to him at breakfast on account of June being there."

"Slocum, June knows everything that's happened up till this. She doesn't need—"

"I really didn't want to tell her about me having Patricia in there," Slocum said.

"I guess you could leave that part out."

"Yeah. I reckon I could at that," said Slocum.

"Why don't you go on and tell Fletcher?" said Glover. "I'll go back to the store and tell June."

"All right."

Back on the main street, the two men parted company, Glover headed for his store and Slocum toward the sheriff's office. When he stepped in, Fletcher looked up from his desk. Pearly was leaning back against the wall on two legs of a straight chair, chewing on a toothpick.

"What can I do for you, Slocum?" the sheriff asked.

Slocum glanced over at Pearly. He did not trust Pearly, but he wasn't sure why. Maybe it was just that he did not like the man.

"Can I see you in private for a minute?" he asked.

Fletcher looked at him for a moment, then stood up. "Let's go have another cup of coffee," he said.

Pearly frowned as the two men left the office. When they shut the door, he walked over to sit behind the sheriff's desk. Outside, Slocum and Fletcher walked along in silence. When they reached the eating place, they found it nearly empty. They got their coffee and took a table a good ways away from the counter. Each man took a sip.

"I lied to you a while ago," Slocum said.

"What about?"

"I didn't want to say nothing in front of June," Slocum explained. "That shot last night. I fired it."

"You?"

"I was in the back room. The door to the back room was open, and I seen a couple of men trying the front door. I took a shot, but it went low. I hit one of them, likely in the lower leg. They got away, but while they were running, I heard one of them say that Thad told him the girl would be in the store."

"Thad? Thad Slater?"

"All he said was Thad."

"I don't know another one around these parts," Elgie said.

"There's a blood trail leading across the street and round behind the bank. Two horses was waiting there. I figured we might could track them today."

Fletcher finished his coffee and stood up.

"Come on, Slocum," he said. "let's go find out."

13

Slocum and Fletcher got their horses and rode around to the back side of the bank, where they picked up the trail of the two would-be store wreckers. It wasn't hard to follow. Not a bit. Now and then, alongside the hoofprints, were a few drops of blood from the wound. They rode out of town in the direction of Sam Slater's ranch. At one point, when it became obvious where they were headed, Slocum and Fletcher gave one another knowing looks, but neither man said a word. They rode on in silence. Soon they found themselves at the main gate of Slater's spread. They paused only briefly, then rode on through.

The tracks they had been following led to the corral. The two horses were just two of Slater's remuda. Any cowhands could have ridden them. But there was the wound. That would not be hard to track. They turned their horses and headed for the main ranch house. It was a good, sturdy house, but not overly impressive or ostentatious. As they slowed their mounts, old Sam Slater himself stepped out onto the porch.

"Howdy, Sheriff," he said. "Slocum, is it?"

"That's right," said Slocum.

"Well, what can I do for you?"

"Two men hit Glover's store again last night, Sam," said Fletcher. "Slocum was there. He drove them off. Shot one of them. Prob'ly in the lower leg. We tracked them here."

"Two of my men, huh?"

"It sure looks like."

"What do you want me to do?"

"Just stay here, Sam. Me and Slocum will amble on over to your bunkhouse and take a look, if you don't mind."

"Help yourselves," said Slater.

Fletcher looked at Slocum and said, "Let's go on over there."

They took a long, slow walk to the bunkhouse, both of them watching the building carefully with each step, in case the two men were watching. No one looked out a window. No one stepped out the door. They reached the bunkhouse and stopped at the front door. Slocum gave Fletcher a look, and Fletcher reached for the door handle. Slocum slipped the Colt out of its holster. Fletcher shoved the door open, and the two men stepped inside, Fletcher pulling out his own six-gun on the way in. A man lying on a bunk and covered up with a blanket sat up with a start.

"Hey," he said, "what is this?"

His hand was a few inches from his gun handle.

"I wouldn't do that, mister," Slocum said.

The man lowered his hand slowly. "What do you want here?" he asked.

"I'm Sheriff Fletcher," said Elgie.

"I know who you are," the man said. "I seen you in town before. What do you want?"

"How come you ain't out working today?" Elgie asked.

"I'm sick. That's all. It ain't too bad."

Slocum stepped up close to the bunk, grabbed the blanket by its edge and jerked it off, exposing a bandaged calf. Blood had soaked through the bandage.

"That what you're sick of?" he asked.

"It was a accident," the man said. "I shot myself. A flesh wound is all. I'll be good as new in a few days."

"Where were you at last night?" asked the sheriff.

"I, uh, I was right here."

"Any witnesses?"

"Well, sure. My pal, Ardie Snow, he was here."

"That's two of you," Elgie said. "Any other witnesses?"

"No. What's wrong? You don't believe me and Ardie? What are you after anyhow?"

"What's your name?"

"I'm Josh Turpin."

"Well, Turpin," said Elgie, "two men tried to break into Larry Glover's store in town last night. Slocum here shot one of them. We followed a blood trail and hoofprints right out here to the corral."

"And then we find you here with a bullet hole in your leg," Slocum added. "What's that add up to in your mind?"

"Now, wait a minute. I never—"

"Who else then?" Slocum said. "Hell, we all know it was you. You and your pal Snow rode into town last night and tried the front door of the store. I fired a low shot through the front door and hit you in the leg. I heard you yelp, and I heard you say that Thad told you that only a girl would be in the store. Then the two of you ran off, across the street and around behind the bank. Your horses were waiting there. You got on them and rode back here as fast as you could go. We followed the prints and we followed your blood trail."

Turpin hung his head and stared at the bed between his legs.

"Well," said Fletcher. "What about it?"

"What do you want me to say?"

"Admit it."

"All right. It was me he shot last night. But I didn't do nothing. I was just standing there by the door. That's all."

"You and who else?"

"I don't remember."

"Was it Ardie Snow?" Slocum asked.

"No."

"Get up," said Fletcher.

"What for?"

"We're going to town."

"I told you I was just there by the door, and—"

"I'm arresting you for conspiring to run the Glovers out of business," said Fletcher, "and for murder."

"Murder? Wait a minute. What murder? I ain't killed no one. You can't pin no murder on me."

"Glover's wagon was wrecked and Charley Jones and Bo Pearson were murdered," Fletcher said. "Later, Glover's store was set on fire. There have been other things, and they're all tied together."

"I didn't have nothing to do with that wagon."

"We'll find out," Fletcher said. "Your tongue will loosen up in jail. Come on."

Slocum grabbed the shoulder of Turpin's shirt and dragged him to his feet. When the outlaw's foot with the bloody bandage on the same leg hit the floor, Turpin began to hop and holler. Slocum shook him hard, and he finally settled down. He pulled on his boots and his britches and hobbled outside. Fletcher nodded toward the corral. "Saddle him up a horse, Slocum. I'll tell Slater we're borrowing it."

Slocum headed for the corral, and Fletcher made Turpin walk over to the porch with him. Turpin limped and whimpered all the way. When they reached the porch, they found old Slater still standing there. He stared down hard at Turpin.

"I sent Slocum to saddle a horse for Turpin here," Fletcher said. "I'll see that it gets returned."

"All right," said Slater.

"I'm taking him in for his attempt on Glover's store last night. I mean to question him about some other things as well. He won't say who he was riding with, though. You got one more guilty party somewhere on your ranch. What do you know about Ardie Snow?"

Slater nodded toward Turpin. "Him and Snow's kinda like partners," he said. "I hired them on together. They hang pretty tight from what all I've seen."

"Do you know where Snow was last night?"

Slater shook his head. "I don't keep much track no more," he said. "I've kinda turned the hard work and all the running of the ranch over to Thad. I'm getting too old myself."

"Where is Thad?"

"He's on a buying trip today, down south of here.

Won't be back for a couple of days. Maybe some time tomorrow. It's hard to tell."

"I'll be wanting to talk to him when he gets back," Fletcher said.

"I'll tell him."

Slocum came leading a saddled horse from the corral, to where Fletcher waited with Turpin and the other horses.

"All right," said Fletcher to Turpin, "mount up."

Turpin winced out loud as he struggled up onto the horse's back. Fletcher mounted his own horse, and Slocum looked from Slater to Fletcher.

"Sheriff," he said, "what about—"

"Never mind, Slocum," Fletcher said. "Come on."

Slocum could not figure why the sheriff did not want to question old Slater further. They had plenty on him. The shots that had killed Jones and Pearson had come from a location on the Slater ranch. The man with the Starr carbine had worked for Slater, and now these two. And Slocum had heard them say that Thad had told them the girl would be in the store. What more did Fletcher want? Well, hell, first things first. He'd wait till they had Turpin in jail, and then he would quiz up Fletcher regarding his motives for going easy on old Slater. Or maybe . . .

"Fletcher," he said.

The sheriff looked around at him. "Yeah?"

"Look, why don't you ride on ahead a little? Leave me here with Turpin. Alone. Just for a little while."

"What for, Slocum?"

"I just got a few questions I want to ask him. In private. That's all."

"I can imagine how you'd ask them, too," said Fletcher. "Forget it."

"I won't do him a serious hurt," Slocum said.

"Sheriff," said Turpin, his voice desperate, "Sheriff, don't do it. Don't leave me here with him. He's crazy. He'll kill me."

Fletcher looked with disgust for a moment at the sniveling Turpin.

"Hell," he said, "why shouldn't I? Maybe he could help

you recall who it was you rode into town with last night."

"All right. All right. It was Ardie all right. Me and Ardie. But like I told you, we didn't do nothing. Just walked up to the door, that's all. We never even opened it."

"You were fixing to," said Slocum.

"Yeah, but we never got a chance. You can't charge us with something we never got to do, can you?"

"I already told you what I'm charging you with, Turpin."

"Me and Ardie didn't have nothing to do with them killings. I done told you that. You can't pin them on us. Hell, we wasn't even working for ole Slater yet when that happened. We wasn't even in this country yet."

"We can check on that," said Fletcher.

"Well, you go on and check away. You'll find I ain't lying none about that."

"Who set you on the store last night?" asked Slocum.

Turpin clamped his lips tight.

"Was it Slater?" said Slocum.

"I ain't saying."

"You said that it was Thad who told you the place wouldn't be guarded. Only the girl would be there."

"That's right. It was Thad what said it. I'll admit to that much only on account a you heard me say it last night."

"Thad Slater?" asked Fletcher.

"Yeah. Thad Slater."

Slocum looked at Elgie. "That's all we need, ain't it?" he said.

"Not quite, Slocum."

"What more then?"

"This bastard could be saying anything that comes into his head."

"I heard him say that Thad—"

"Slocum," said Fletcher, "let it go for now. Sam told us that Thad would be home in a couple of days. It'll wait till then."

Slocum did not like it, but he kept quiet for the rest of the trip back into town. The sheriff headed straight for the jail with Turpin, and Slocum headed for Glover's store. He couldn't think of anything else to do except plan his next trip, the one that was calculated to draw out the culprits. There really was no merchandise to be picked up. Slocum was just going to take out a wagon in hopes that someone would try for it. It was meant to be a trap.

Back at the store, he told Glover what had happened and what they had found out.

"You think Slater's behind it then?" Glover asked.

"It sure looks that way to me," said Slocum.

"Why do you think Elgie's holding off?"

"He wants to talk to Thad, he says."

"Well, he may be right about that," said Larry. "Thad might have some explanation, or even if he's guilty, he could be doing it without ole Sam's knowledge. I understand that Sam has more or less retired, left everything up to Thad to run."

"Yeah. That's what he said."

They talked then about Slocum's trip the next day. Slocum could see no reason to cancel or postpone it. If anything was going to happen, it would likely happen on the first day out.

"Might as well go ahead," he said. "Be one way for me to pass the time till Thad gets back."

"All right," said Glover. "When do you mean to take off?"

"First thing in the morning," said Slocum.

When Slocum came around in the morning to drive the wagon out of town, the first thing that he heard was that someone had fired through the window of the jail the night before and killed the prisoner, Turpin. Now, that really was a wrinkle. Who the hell knew that Turpin had been arrested? Old Slater, that's who. Then he had to slow his thinking. Someone could have seen them bring Turpin in, and Slater might have said something to some of his cowhands. Surely, Snow had missed his buddy when he returned to the bunkhouse—if he had returned. Hell, Slocum had to admit to himself that the whole mess was as much a mess as it had ever been, and he wasn't sure of a damn thing. Well, maybe his fake trip would flush something out.

He made a big show of driving the wagon to the front of the store and standing out on the sidewalk with Larry Glover, talking and looking at a piece of paper. After some time, he folded the paper and tucked it inside his shirt. At last, he climbed onto the wagon seat, lifted the reins and, with a flick of them, started the wagon to rolling.

14

Slocum drove out from Mesa Poquita again, riding the same road he had ridden before, the road that would take him to Denver, if he stayed on it long enough. This time, though, he had no intention of staying out that long. He left town in the wagon boldly in the early morning daylight, making sure that plenty of folks saw him go. For a ways, he wasn't worried about anything happening, but when he reached the spot in the road where Jones and Pearson had been killed, he began to be cautious, watching all around for any possible ambush. It could happen anywhere along the way. He knew that. There had been another killing now, and he was certain that, whatever the motives, whoever the culprit, they would stop at nothing.

Elgie Fletcher rode out to Slater's ranch to confront the old man once again. As usual, Slater came out on the porch when he heard the approach of a horse. Fletcher stopped a few feet from the porch. He nodded, still sitting in the saddle. "Morning, Sam," he said.

"Two days in a row," said Slater. "I'm beginning to feel popular, or at least important."

"You mind if I climb down and visit a spell?" said Fletcher.

"Come on," said Slater. "Visit away. I got nothing much to do with my time anyway. Cup of coffee?"

"No, thanks, Sam," said Fletcher as he swung down out of the saddle. "This ain't a social call."

As he walked on up to the porch, Slater sat down in a straight wooden chair and indicated another for Fletcher to take. Fletcher sat down and heaved a sigh.

"Sam," he said, "last night someone killed Josh Turpin in the jail cell. Shot him through the window. My deputy was sleeping right in the office."

"That's too bad," Slater said. "Did Pearly see the man?"

"By the time Pearly jumped up and figured out what the hell had happened, the killer was long gone."

"You ain't figuring that I had anything to do with it, are you?"

"Sam, we been friends a lot of years. I don't want to think anything bad about you, but there are a number of things about this whole mess pointing straight out here to your ranch."

"Thad's hired on a few men lately that I don't know," said Slater. "Hell, he don't even know them. Drifters. That's what they are. We was short of hands, and we had to take what come along."

"I know that. But you got to look at it from my way of seeing. First off, Charlie Jones and Bo Pearson was shot from your ranch. Then that Starr rifle belonged to one of your hands. And last night, Slocum caught another one of your boys trying to break into Glover's store. That Turpin. Turpin told us that his partner last night was Ardie Snow, and I think he'da told me more than that, but someone stopped him."

"Stopped him good from what you said."

"Yeah."

"Do you expect me to start in defending myself, Elgie? 'Cause I ain't got no reason. I don't know a damned thing about all this shit. You know as well as I do that anyone could ride onto my ranch without my knowledge and set up yonder in them rocks and pick off someone riding along the road. And you know that them hands Thad hired on was strangers to us. Just what is it you're expecting of me?"

"I don't know, Sam," said Fletcher, shaking his head

real slow. "I don't know. I come out here to talk to you, and I want to talk to that Ardie Snow. Where can I find him?"

"Your guess is as good as mine," Slater said. "After you left here yesterday, you and that Slocum feller, I called in Justin Morgan and asked him to send Snow over here. He said Snow was gone. He didn't leave no word. But he was gone with all of his gear."

"He's gone?" said Fletcher.

" 'Fraid so. Say, there's Justin over by the corral. You want to talk to him?"

"Yeah. I might as well."

Slater hollered out to his foreman, and Morgan rode over to the porch. He tipped his hat to Slater and to the sheriff. "What is it, Mr. Slater?" he asked. "Any trouble?"

"Come on up here on the porch and set," Slater said. Morgan dismounted and found himself a chair on the porch. He looked at Slater and Fletcher with curiosity.

"Justin," said Slater, "my old friend the sheriff here suspicions me of being involved with them attacks on the Glovers."

"I never said that, Sam."

"Not straight out, you didn't. Anyhow, he come looking for that Snow feller, and I told him what you said."

"He just took off sometime yesterday," Morgan said. "He didn't say nothing to me or anyone else. None of the hands know anything, or if they do, they ain't saying."

"Snow, Turpin . . ."

"They was all part of that bunch Thad hired when we was so shorthanded," said Morgan, interrupting the sheriff. "They had all come riding into town together looking for work, they said. They'd been hanging around a couple of days by the time he met them, so he figured they was serious and hired them on."

"You mean, they were all acquainted with each other?" Fletcher asked.

"Yes, sir," said Morgan. "Like I said, they rode in together."

Elgie took off his hat and scratched his head, looking

at the porch floor. "Damn," he said. "Are any of that bunch still around?"

"Snow was the last of them," Morgan said.

"We're shorthanded again," added Slater.

"Well, I'd suggest you be careful who you hire on," Fletcher said.

"One thing you might ought to consider, Elgie," said Slater.

"What's that?"

"This trouble all started when that Slocum come riding in here. Didn't it?"

Elgie Fletcher headed back toward town more puzzled than ever. If that bunch of so-called cowhands had ridden into Mesa Poquita together, if they had all been buddies, then the whole thing must have been planned well ahead of time. Then whoever it was who was behind it all must have sent for them. But who could that be? Sam Slater? Thad? Slocum? Elgie did not feel like he was any closer to the answer than he had ever been. Now the only person he knew of who was still alive to talk had vanished. Where the hell could Ardie Snow have gone? Had he bailed out and left the country, or was he up to something? It was pretty clear that after Slocum had shot Turpin in the leg, Snow must have figured that they were getting too close for comfort, so he had gone into a hole somewhere. Elgie then wondered if it had been Snow who had killed Turpin last night. Maybe, he thought. Maybe.

He rounded a corner in the road that headed toward town. There were trees on both sides of the road, thick with brush underneath. Elgie saw the flash of a rifle barrel but too late. Flame sprang out from the barrel and a shot rang out. The bullet smashed into Elgie's chest an instant later, and he slumped in the saddle. A low moan escaped from his lips. The horse continued on its journey toward town, the man in the saddle sagging and bouncing loosely as it went.

Slocum was getting nervous. He figured that someone should have tried something before this. He was well away from town, beyond the spot where Jones and Pearson had been killed. What were they waiting for? he wondered. He was approaching a stretch of road where a wall rose up to his left. The hillside was spotted with boulders and clumps of scrubby trees and brush. He kept his eyes on the possible hiding places along the way. Then a rifle shot sounded, and a slug tore into the wagon seat just beside him. A too hasty shot, he thought. Not bothering to stop the wagon, Slocum grabbed his Winchester and threw himself out and onto the road. He hit the ground rolling and flung himself into the ditch on the left side of the road. Someone with a rifle was somewhere up above him. He cranked a shell into the chamber of the Winchester and waited, scouring the hillside all the while for any telltale signs—a puff of smoke, a movement, anything. There was nothing.

Suddenly a man about halfway up the hill appeared from behind a tree and ran in a crouch toward a nearby boulder. Slocum fired two rapid shots from his Winchester, both of them kicking up dust at the man's boot heels. "Damn," he said. He had been surprised and had fired too quickly, but at least now he knew where the son of a bitch was. He trained his sights on the boulder, waiting for the man to make another move. It was quiet again. Ahead on the road, the horses pulling the wagon had at last realized that no one was driving them, and they had ambled to a stop.

Impatient, Slocum fired a shot at the boulder, kicking up shards of rock. The man stayed down, hidden from view. It was a tough situation, a standoff. If Slocum moved from the ditch, the man would have a good shot at him. If the man moved from behind the boulder, Slocum would be able to pick him off. "Hell," Slocum muttered to himself, "we could just lay here and starve to death like this."

Then he noticed, almost directly above and behind the man, a jutting rock. Three or four feet protruded out from the dirt of the hillside. There were other rocks around it. It shoved itself out from a kind of cluster of smaller rocks. Slocum wondered how much of the rock was still in the ground. He sighted in on it and fired. A few loose rocks tumbled down the hillside. Some of them must have landed on the man below, but if so, he made no move or sound. Slocum fired again. More rocks fell, and this time the larger, jutting rock seemed to slip a little. He fired again. The rock dropped some. It was loose. It shouldn't take much more.

He fired once more, and the great rock came loose, plunging down toward Slocum's target, but the man had figured what Slocum was up to, and he ran from behind the boulder just in time. Slocum tried a shot at the man, but it hit behind him. Then the man lost his footing and fell hard on his butt. He kept his grip on his rifle though, as he started to slide down the side of the hill on his backside. "God damn," he shouted. Slocum stood to take aim at the man, but the man turned his body and started rolling. He rolled to the bottom of the hillside and fell into the same ditch Slocum was in. The road curved a bit, and the two men could not see one another.

Slocum figured the man was in the ditch about even with where the horses and wagon had stopped. He considered dropping back down onto his belly and inching forward in the ditch until he could see the man, but then the man might see him coming first. It would be a chancy thing to try. He looked up the side of the hill and saw that there was cover not far above and just a little ahead of him. It was a small rock just in front of a clump of brush. He decided to try for it.

Crouching, he ran for the cover. The climb was steeper than he had expected, and he slipped once, but he did not lose his footing. He kept going. He was only a few feet from his goal when a rifle shot clipped his boot heel. He made a headlong dive and snuggled in behind the rock. Another shot hit the rock. Slocum stood up quickly. The man was standing in the ditch below. Slocum raised his rifle and fired rapidly, three shots. He could see that at least one shot hit the mark, as the man twisted from the impact and the pain, then dropped his own rifle and sank down in the ditch. Slocum moved out cautiously. He knew that the man was hurt, but he did not know how badly. Perhaps he could still fire his weapon.

As he moved down the hill, Slocum kept watching, but the man did not rise again. Slocum slowed his pace even more when he reached the bottom of the hillside and moved toward the ditch. Peering over, he saw the man writhing in pain. He saw the blood over the man's chest. He was sure that it had been a death shot. He stepped down into the ditch and picked up the man's rifle, which he tossed aside. Then he reached for the six-gun at the man's side, pulled it out of the holster and tossed it after the rifle.

"God damn you," the man said.

"You was trying to do the same thing to me," Slocum said.

"I wish I had."

"What's your name, mister?" Slocum asked.

"What do you care?"

"I like to know who it is I've killed."

"Figure it out, you son of a bitch."

The man died. Slocum checked to make sure. Then he straightened up again, said, "Shit" and started dragging the body out of the ditch to load it into the wagon.

Thad Slater got off the stage in Mesa Poquita. He said hello to a couple of people on the street as he passed on his way to the livery where he had left his horse. At the livery, he paid the man and had him saddle his horse. Then, hanging his valise on the saddle horn, he mounted up and rode over to Larry Glover's store. Leaving his horse and his valise at the hitchrail, he went inside. Millie saw him as he stepped into the store. She smiled.

"Hi, Thad," she said.

"Hello, Millie. I just got back in, and I wanted to stop and see you before I went on out to the ranch."

"I'm glad you did," she said.

"How've you been?"

"Oh, busy, but that's all right. I like it that way. How was your trip?"

"I'd say it was successful. I have to get on home to tell

Dad about it. Like I said, I just wanted to see you first.
I'll come calling in a day or two, if it's all right."

"I wish you would," she said. And she started to say,
I missed you, but thought better of it. Instead, she just
smiled.

Thad left the store and mounted up to ride back to the
ranch. He'd had a successful trip, having bought a new
string of horses which would be delivered to the ranch in
a few more days. He was anxious to get home and tell
the old man. He rode along in a good mood until he came
to a curve in the road where trees grew on both sides, and
in the shadow of the trees, in the middle of the road, he
saw a horse standing and, beside the horse, the body of a
man. He rode ahead quickly, vaulting out of the saddle
when he reached the prone figure. He could see blood on
the man's back. He could tell that the man was dead, even
before he touched the corpse.

He reached carefully for a shoulder and rolled the carcass over, and then he saw that it was Elgie Fletcher. "Oh,
God," he said. He loaded the body onto the horse, turned
his own horse around and headed back toward town.

15

When Slocum arrived back in Mesa Poquita with the body of the bushwhacker in the back of the wagon, he saw a crowd gathered around the sheriff's office. Something must have happened, he thought. He hoped that it had something to do with the trouble that Glover was having. He drove on over and stopped, setting the brake and climbing down. Then he shoved his way through the crowd. Suddenly he stopped, for there on the sidewalk was the body of Elgie Fletcher. Pearly was standing there talking with Thad Slater. Slocum stared at the body in near disbelief.

"Well, Slocum," said Pearly. "Just the man I wanted to see."

"What's happened?" Slocum asked.

"It's clear enough, ain't it?" snapped Pearly. "Someone's killed Elgie. That's what."

"I found him out on the road," said Thad. "I was on my way home."

"That's enough," said Pearly. "Thad, you can go on home. I don't need nothing more from you right now. Slocum, come on into the office."

Slocum followed Pearly into the sheriff's office. Pearly moved directly behind Fletcher's big desk, sat down, leaned back and propped his feet on the desk.

"All right, Slocum," he said, "just what the hell do you know about this?"

"I don't know a damn thing," Slocum said. "I was coming here to see him."

"What about?"

"I was bringing in a body," Slocum said.

"Another body?" said Pearly, dropping his feet to the floor and sitting up straight. "Where is it?"

"Out there in the wagon."

Pearly was out the door in a flash. By the time Slocum reached the doorway the deputy was staring into the wagon bed. He turned around to look back at Slocum with a wrinkled-up nose and a quizzical expression on his face. "Who the hell was he?" he asked.

"Damned if I know," Slocum said. "He tried to ambush me out on the road this morning. I got him instead."

"Damn it," said Pearly. "Hiram, here's another one."

The undertaker, who was kneeling over the remains of the sheriff, glanced up. "All right, Pearly," he said.

A cowhand who was standing in the small crowd elbowed his way forward and stepped over to the wagon, looking inside. "Hey," he said, "it's that damned Ardie Snow."

Pearly looked at the cowhand for a moment, then stomped back into the office. Slocum stepped aside to let him pass, then followed him back in and shut the door. Once inside with the door shut, Pearly stalked around the office as if in deep thought. Then he turned suddenly on Slocum. "You said you don't know nothing about what happened to Elgie," he said.

"That's right."

"How the hell do I know that?"

"Did I hear young Slater say he found the body on the road on his way home?" Slocum asked.

"Yeah. That's right."

"When did you last see Fletcher?"

"This morning," said Pearly. "Just before he rode out toward Slater's ranch."

"Well, hell, you and everyone else saw me drive out the north road this morning. How could I know what happened on the road to the Slater place?"

"Well, shit, that's right," said Pearly. "Aw, hell, Slocum, what's going on around here? I can't figger this damn thing out. And it looks like I'm the sheriff here now, at least till they can call up a new election."

"Pearly, you don't seem to me to be too bright, so I'm going to explain this to you real slow and easy. Someone's out to ruin the Glovers. We don't know who it is. They killed Jones and Pearson. They tried to burn the store. They tried to stop me out on the road twice. Night before last, they tried again at the store, but I shot one of them. That turned out to be ole Turpin, and they killed him in the jail last night just to keep him quiet. Now I expect they decided that Elgie Fletcher was a little too smart for them or getting a little too close to the truth, and so they killed him, too. Does any of that make any sense to you?"

"Well, yeah. I guess so. But who the hell could it be?" Pearly had suddenly gone from a bombastic, swaggering son of a bitch to a whimpering snip. Slocum thought it was somehow amusing.

"I don't know that, Pearly. Me and Elgie went out to talk to Slater, but we didn't have enough to do anything."

"What did you have?"

"Jones and Pearson were shot from a location on Slater's ranch," said Slocum. "All the cowhands that we've caught or killed had been working for Slater. When they were trying to break into the store, Turpin told Snow that Thad told him just the girl would be there. Then Elgie was killed on his way either to or from Slater's ranch. I'd say it looks pretty bad for the Slaters."

"Well, I reckon I had ought to go out there and arrest them then," said Pearly.

"I felt that way, too," said Slocum, "till Elgie straightened me out. Anyone could have gone onto the ranch to fire them shots. The cowhands was all strangers to the Slaters when Thad hired them, and anyone could have ambushed Elgie out there on the road. The worst thing is what I said about Thad—what Turpin said."

"That Thad had told him the girl was in the store?"

"That's it. If you hadn't sent Thad home a while ago, we could have asked him about that."

"Let's go out there and talk to him," said Pearly. "You want to ride out there with me?"

"Make it in about an hour," said Slocum. "I'll ride out with you."

Slocum left the sheriff's office and walked over to the store. He found June and Larry both in. June was busy with a customer, but Larry walked over to join Slocum.

"I didn't expect you back so soon," he said.

"I was ambushed all right," Slocum said. "It was Ardie Snow, and I killed him. I didn't know it was Snow, though, till a cowhand identified him over at the sheriff's office just now."

"So we haven't learned anything?"

"That's right. Have you heard yet? Someone killed the sheriff this morning, too."

"What? Elgie?"

"It was on the road to Slater's ranch."

"My God, Slocum. All this because of me? I think I'd better sell out. Patton has made me an offer. It's not what I should get for the place, but it would be enough for me and June to pack up and try to start over somewhere else."

"Why would you want to do that?" Slocum asked.

"To stop all this killing," said Glover. "We're no closer to knowing who's responsible for it now than we were the first day you rode in here."

"Well, you're right about that," Slocum admitted, "but if you quit, whoever it is wins, and he's an evil man. I wouldn't want to see that happen."

"But Slocum—"

Larry caught himself. He paused, looking in the direction of June and her customer. He took Slocum by an arm and made a move toward the door. "Let's go outside," he said. Slocum followed him out. Larry looked up and down the sidewalk. There was no one anywhere near.

"Slocum," he said, "the way things are going, something could happen to June. I'd never forgive myself if that happened."

"I can understand that, Larry, but suppose you give June the choice."

"Aw, she'll stick, Slocum. You know that, and I know it."

"Then why don't you do as much as your wife will do?"

"Damn it, Slocum—"

"Look, Larry, let's give it a little longer. A few more days. Okay?"

"All right," said Glover. "We'll see."

The customer June had been dealing with came out of the store. Larry nodded to her. Slocum said, "Let's go back in. We can't be keeping any of this news from June." As Slocum and Glover stepped back into the store, Millie came walking out of the bank on her way back from an errand. She almost bumped into Patricia Patton.

"Oh, excuse me," she said.

"Oh, that's all right," Patricia said. "It's Millie, isn't it?"

"That's right, and you're Patricia Patton. I remember you from the dance."

"You were with Thad Slater," said Patricia. "Hey, he's a good catch."

"Oh, I haven't caught him," said Millie. "He just took me to the dance. That's all."

"Don't be modest. Thad's the best catch around. I'd be jealous if I was going to stay around these parts."

"Are you leaving?" said Millie.

Patricia shrugged. "It won't be long now," she said. "Daddy and I are going to be moving to San Francisco. There will be lots of boys from good families out there. I'll make me a good match."

"I hope everything works out well for you," Millie said. "If you'll excuse me, I have to get back to work."

Slocum and Pearly rode together out to Slater's ranch, and by the time they got there, Slocum had decided that Pearly wasn't such a bad egg after all. He was just a bit slow. He didn't talk too much on the road, and when he did, he asked almost sensible questions. The main thing, though, was that Pearly obviously knew that he was dealing with something that was way over his head, and he was letting Slocum call the shots.

When they arrived at the ranch, he said just enough to

let the Slaters know that he and Slocum were there on official business. From there, once again, he let Slocum take the lead. They were sitting in the living room in the Slater ranch house. Sam and Thad were both there.

"Well, uh, Slocum here has got a couple of questions for you, I believe," Pearly said.

"Just one," Slocum corrected.

"Fire away," said Thad.

"I was in the store alone when Turpin and Snow tried to break in," Slocum said. "I heard one of them say that Thad had told him the girl would be there alone."

"That's not a question," said Thad.

"Can you explain it?" Pearly said, frowning.

"No. I can't," said Thad. "I might have said that, or something like it. I know now that Millie has moved into the hotel, and with what all has been happening at the store, I'm glad of it. But that night at the dance, I didn't know it. She met me at the store, you recall, and she didn't say anything about having made a move. I know that Turpin was at the dance, and I think Snow was there, too, but I'm not sure. I was worried about Millie staying at the store, and I might have said something about it where Turpin overheard. I can't really say."

Slocum sat staring at Thad. The funny thing was—he believed him. He couldn't say why. He just believed him. He went over in his mind all the things that seemed to add up and point the finger at the Slaters, and he dismissed them all one at a time as circumstantial. He explained each one away. The main thing in Slocum's mind in favor of the Slaters was just that Slocum believed what Thad had said. He decided, however, to keep it to himself for the time being.

"Thad," he said, "did you know any of the cowhands you hired the last time around?"

"That's another question," Thad said. "You said you had only one."

"One thing leads to another," said Slocum.

"Answer the question, Thad," said Pearly.

"Take it easy, Pearly," Slocum said.

"All right," said Thad. "I went to town one day. We were shorthanded, and someone told me that there were a half dozen cowhands over at the saloon. They'd been hanging around for a few days. They said they were all looking for work. I talked to them for a while, and then I hired them. I had never seen any of them before."

"Did you get a recommendation from anyone?" asked Slocum.

"They said they had all worked for the Circle Q out west of here," said Thad. "I wrote a letter. Haven't got any response yet. In the meantime, Patton gave them a recommendation—sort of. He said they'd been hanging around his place, and they seemed like a pretty good bunch of guys. He kind of asked me to give them a chance while I waited for the letter."

"Patton, huh?" said Slocum.

"Yeah. That's three questions I've answered."

"Well, I have one more. How'd your trip go?"

"It went pretty good," Thad said. "I bought a nice string of horses. They'll be delivered here in a few days."

"Well, we've bothered you enough," Slocum said, standing up. Pearly stood, too. "We'll be running along."

Old man Slater stood up with a groan. "Sure you won't have a glass of whiskey with us?" he asked.

"Maybe next time," Slocum said.

"Well, come around anytime," the old man said. "Hell, I like having someone to talk to, even if he is accusing me of something."

"We'll be in touch," said Slocum.

"Yeah," said Pearly, and he followed Slocum out the door.

On the trail several miles away from Mesa Poquita, a man in black sat beside a camp fire sipping coffee. His black horse stood grazing nearby. The man put the coffee cup down on the ground beside him and reached inside his shirt to pull out a folded piece of paper. He turned the paper slightly so it would catch the light from the fire, and he read.

I hired some cowhands at cheap wages to do the job for me, but they failed miserably. I won't insult you with the same kind of offer I made to them. I'll pay you well. Half the cash. And there is a bundle, I assure you. As I told you before, there is at least a million dollars worth of gold involved. When you get to town, act like you don't know me. I'll get word to you somehow at the saloon.

The man in black smiled, folded the letter back up and tucked it inside his shirt. He picked up his coffee cup and sipped.

16

For the next three days, Slocum hung around the store and slept the nights there. Nothing out of the ordinary happened. There were no more attacks on the store. It seemed almost as if there were no problem. Slocum began to feel nervous. He knew that something was bound to happen sooner or later. He wished that it would be sooner. Just waiting around like this was eating on his nerves. He didn't like it. It did make a little sense, though. Because he knew now that Slocum was staying at the store, whoever was behind all this was afraid to try anything more there.

Slocum went for breakfast one morning with the Glovers. Millie joined them. They sat sipping coffee waiting for their breakfast. It seemed like they were all avoiding saying anything at all about what was surely on all their minds. Millie finally said, "You know, tomorrow is my day off."

"Yes," said June. "Do you have any plans?"

Millie ducked her head. "Thad Slater is coming by to take me out for a ride," she said. Slocum looked up from his coffee, and Millie caught his eye. "There's no harm in it," she said. "Don't look at me like that, Slocum."

"I didn't say anything," Slocum said.

"But I saw the way you were looking at me. Thad's a nice boy, and I have a right to have a little fun now and then. Well, don't I?"

"Of course you do, Millie," said June, reaching across the table to give Millie's hand a pat. "You just go on and have a good time."

Just then Patton and his daughter walked in, and June spoke to them. They paused there beside the table. June invited them to sit down.

"We've got plenty of room here," she said.

The two Pattons sat. "So," said Patton, "how's life been treating you two Glovers?"

"Things have been pretty quiet for the last few days," Larry said.

"Business has been good," said June. "If things go on like this, we should get caught up again in a short while."

"Good," said Patton. "I'm glad to hear it. You two have already had more trouble than anyone ought to have to put up with. Let's hope things go smoothly from here on out."

"I don't think we can relax quite so soon," said Larry. "Whoever it is who's been after us ain't going to quit just like that."

"He seems to have quit," said Patton. "That's a good sign, I'd say. What do you think, Slocum?"

"I'd say it's a sign that something's going to happen," said Slocum, "and if we don't stay alert, it'll happen when we least expect it."

Glover nodded his head in agreement, but Patricia said, "Oh, Slocum, that's just being grim."

"Yeah," said Patton. "Maybe you being here has scared them off—whoever they are."

"Maybe," said Glover.

"I wouldn't count on that," Slocum said.

The waiter brought coffee cups for the Pattons and poured refills for the rest. Then he took the Pattons' orders and went on about his business. Slocum glanced over at Patricia, but she remained very composed, not giving a hint that anything had ever passed between them. He was glad enough of that. It felt a little strange, though, sitting at the same table with her and her father.

"So what are your plans?" Patton asked.

Glover shot a glance at Slocum, and Slocum shrugged.

"Ain't much planning we can do," said Slocum.

"Business as usual," Glover added.

"Well, I guess it's none of my business," said Patton, "but if it was me getting all that harassment, I don't believe I'd just sit around waiting for something else to happen."

"What would you be doing, Patton?" said Slocum.

"Well, I—"

"Can't we think of a better subject of breakfast conversation?" said Patricia, interrupting her father. "All this kind of talk is not very good for my appetite, and I'm sure it won't be good for my digestion."

"Patricia," said Patton, in a tone of admonishment, but before he could say more, June interrupted him.

"I think Patricia's right," she said. "Let's talk of something else."

The waiter brought the meals, and the conversation sort of stopped while everyone busied themselves with their food. The new silence, though, was a little tense. When they had all finished eating, Patton stood up to leave. Patricia stood with him.

"I'm glad that things are going well for you," Patton said to Larry and June. "And I hope that Slocum's assessment of the situation is wrong. We'll be seeing you later."

"See you," said Glover.

"Good day," said June. Millie nodded politely, and Patricia at last gave Slocum a look and a smile. "Be seeing you," she said. Slocum gave her a noncommittal nod and let it go at that.

Slocum hung around the store that day, helping Larry when he could: moving stock around, occasionally loading a customer's purchases into a wagon, but there really wasn't all that much for him to do. The customers came in with fair regularity, but never were there too many of them for June and Millie to handle. Now and then a male came in who went to Larry for help, but Slocum was mostly marking time.

"I think I'll go out and smoke," he said to Larry.

"Sure," said Larry. "You don't need to be hanging around here anyhow, Slocum. We're doing all right."

Slocum went out on the sidewalk and sat down on a straight chair. He pulled out a cigar and lit it. He was wondering and worrying about the seeming calm that had settled in. He tried to assess it. It could be that he had thwarted their attempts so often that they were laying low and trying to figure out their next move. That was a possibility. Another thing that occurred to him was that whoever was behind it all had run out of hired men to do his dirty work. If that was the case, he'd be looking for more hard cases, and sooner or later, he'd find some. They were a dime a dozen in these parts. Slocum was sure of one thing only. The bastard, whoever it was, had not given up. Not just like that.

Slocum glanced up and down the street. What was it, he wondered, about Glover's store? What could anyone possibly be after? Whoever it was was damn sure serious, serious as hell. He'd not just committed three murders and gotten a number of gunnies killed, but one of the men he had murdered was a sheriff.

The Glovers had a good business going. That was for sure. But if someone was just out to take business away from them, he could easily open another store and give them some competition. It couldn't be just that. Had Larry Glover made himself a deadly enemy somehow? They had already tried to answer that question and had come up empty. It just did not seem as if he had any enemies in the whole world. So what the hell could be at the bottom of all this?

It could hardly be the location of the store. The building was sound enough and adequate for its purpose, but it was just another building in a small town. The lot was small, not much more than was needed for the building to fit on, and its location was nothing special. Mesa Poquita was a small town, and there was plenty of room around for any new business that anyone might want to put up. None of it made any sense.

Slocum was sitting there pondering the whole peculiar situation when a stranger came riding into town. Slocum paid particular attention to the man. He called attention to himself just by his appearance. He was riding a black horse, and he was dressed all in black. Slocum noticed particularly the two Colts that were strapped to the man's thighs. He rode easy, not looking one way or the other, but when he arrived at the saloon, he angled his horse over to the hitching rail and dismounted slowly and deliberately. He tied the horse to the rail and went inside.

It was early in the day for a drink, but the man could have been looking for a room. Slocum had heard that there were some rooms upstairs in the place, though Patton did not seem to advertise them. Most of that kind of business went to the hotel. There was something about the stranger that was familiar to Slocum. Not that Slocum had ever seen him before, but he was a type that Slocum knew only too well. He had the look and the manner of a professional killer. Slocum could not help but think that the man might be the latest to be brought in by the one who had been harassing the Glovers. His curiosity got the better of him. He stood up and started walking toward the sheriff's office.

As he stepped into the office, a nervous Pearly jumped up to greet him. "Slocum," he said, "what can I do for you?"

"Sit down, Pearly, and relax," Slocum said. "I just want a gander at all the dodgers you have."

"Oh, sure," said Pearly. He opened a desk drawer and pulled out a stack of papers while Slocum glanced casually at the wanted posters that were hanging on the wall. Slocum moved a chair over beside the big desk and sat down. He picked up the stack of dodgers and started flipping through it. A time or two, he paused to study one, then discarded it with the rest. At last he had gone through the entire stack. He shoved them back across the desk to Pearly.

"That's all of them?" he asked.

"Yes, sir," said Pearly. "That's every last one. Even the ones that come in today's mail."

"All right."

"Mr. Slocum?"

"Yeah?"

"What you looking for?"

"A stranger just rode into town that I'm curious about," Slocum said. "Right now that's all."

"You didn't find him in there, did you?"

"Nope. I didn't really expect to though."

"Well, well, Slocum, what do you want me to do? Do you want me to—"

"Don't do anything just yet," Slocum said. "Sit tight. I'll let you know if I find anything out."

"But this stranger, he's a . . . he's a . . ."

"He's a gunfighter, Pearly," said Slocum. "I can tell that just by looking at him."

"What are you going to do?"

"Watch him," said Slocum, "and wait."

"But he might—"

"He might be just passing through." As Slocum left the office he thought, *Fat chance. The son of a bitch is here up to no good. You can damn well bet on that.* He glanced toward the saloon as he walked back to the store. It would be too obvious to go right on over to the Whistle Stop so soon after the man had arrived. The black horse was still tied up in front, so the stranger was still in there all right. Slocum wondered if the man was meeting with someone. If so, he'd sure as hell like to know who it was. It was difficult to act as if he were minding his own business, but he felt like that was all he could do. He found the chair outside the store still unoccupied, so he sat down in it once more. He kept his eye on the Whistle Stop.

In another few minutes, Glover stepped outside. "What's up, Slocum?" he asked. "I saw you walk over to the sheriff's office."

"Maybe nothing," Slocum said. "See that black horse over there at the Whistle Stop?"

"Yeah. What—"

"A stranger just rode into town on it. He has all the look of a professional gunfighter."

Inside the Whistle Stop, the stranger sat at a table all alone. There was no one else in the place. He sat in silence waiting. In another few minutes, Pat Patton walked out from the back room. He stopped in surprise at the sight of the man.

"Oh," he said, "excuse me. I didn't realize anyone was in here. There's usually not this time of day. What can I do for you?"

"I just rode into town," said the stranger. "I'd like a cup of coffee. Then I'd like to have my horse taken care of, and I'd like to get a room. Do you have rooms here?"

"Yes, I do," Patton said. He went behind the bar and poured a cup of coffee, which he took to the stranger's table. Then he went back to the counter and brought a book out. He laid it on the table for the man to sign. "If you'll just sign here," he said, "I'll give you a room key. Then I'll take care of your horse myself." He handed the man a pen.

The man wrote in the book and shoved it back across the table toward Patton, who picked it up and read, "Broderick Marley." He placed a key on the table near Marley's hand.

"That's number six," he said. "Just at the top of the steps."

"Can I get a bath?"

"I'll have that taken care of right away."

"Take care of the horse first."

"Yes, sir."

"It's the black out front."

"I'll take care of it right away."

Slocum was still watching the front of the Whistle Stop when Patton came hurrying out, untied the black and started leading it toward the livery stable. Without looking up at Glover, he said, "It looks like the stranger is here to stay for a while."

"Yeah," said Glover.

"I'll wait till Patton's business picks up some," Slocum said. "Then I'll take me a walk over there and see if I can find out anything."

"Well, you be careful. Don't start anything with that man. You said that he's a professional gunfighter."

"Hell, Larry, I don't ever start anything. You ought to know that by now."

"Well, even if he starts it, you still be careful."

Slocum laughed. "Don't worry," he said. "I'll just go over and have a drink or two and keep my eyes and ears open. That's all."

"That better be all," said Glover. "I sure don't want you getting killed over this business. I wouldn't want that on my conscience."

"Hey, Larry," Slocum said, "it's not too busy in the store just now. Let's go have us a cup of coffee."

Larry looked at Slocum suspiciously. "Where at?" he said.

Slocum laughed again.

"Well, hell," he said, "not at the damn Whistle Stop."

17

Broderick Marley had had three cups of coffee by the time Patton had his bath ready in the room. His horse had already been stabled. Marley asked Patton if he could have his clothes cleaned, and Patton said of course. Then Marley stood up slowly and made his way to the room followed by a groveling Patton. In the room the gunfighter checked the bath and found it satisfactory. He hung his hat on a peg and sat down to pull off his boots. Then he undressed and handed the suit of clothes to Marley. Patton hustled out of the room, shutting the door behind himself. Marley took off his underwear and, placing his guns on a chair near the tub, climbed in and slowly sank down until the water was up to his chin. With a big sigh, he relaxed.

Slocum and Glover were just going into the eating place for their coffee when they saw Patton hurrying out of the Whistle Stop with the bundle of black clothes. They paused long enough to let him come about even with them. Then, "What's your hurry, Patton?" Slocum said.

"I've got to get these clothes cleaned right away," Patton answered.

"You going someplace special?" said Slocum.

"What? No. They're not mine. I've got a guest."

"A paying guest?"

"Yeah. I've got to go now."

"Well, who is it?" said Glover.

"He signed the register 'Broderick Marley,' " said Patton. "I'm sorry, fellows, but I really have to get going."

Glover laughed as Patton hurried on toward the cleaners. Slocum just stared after the man. Then the two men turned and walked on into the eating place. As they walked toward a table, Glover said to the waiter, "Just coffee." They found a table and sat down, and the waiter brought the coffee over. He put it on the table and left.

"I've never seen Pat rush around like that before," said Glover, still smiling.

"Maybe he's got good reason," said Slocum, lifting his coffee cup for a tentative sip. Glover eyed him with curiosity.

"What do you mean?" he said.

"Could be he's got a real special guest."

"Slocum, what are you getting at?"

"Could be that waiting game we've been playing is about to come to an end."

"Talk plain, Slocum."

"I've heard about Broderick Marley."

"And?"

"Broderick Marley is a paid killer, Larry. He'd gun his own mother if someone paid him to do it. He's as cold-blooded as they come."

"Then why isn't he in jail?"

"He's careful. He's never been caught doing a murder. It's always either on the sly or else he prods the other fellow into going for a gun—first. And he's never been known to miss."

"And you think that he's here to—"

"Could be he's just passing through, but I doubt it."

"But why would our man go to the expense of hiring a professional like that? I mean, he's already killed three men, and one of them the sheriff."

"That's a good question, Larry," Slocum said. "I don't like to brag, but the only thing I can think of is me."

"You?"

"I've managed to upset his applecart most of the time, and I've got rid of his gang of paid bullies. Could be he brought Marley in here to get me out of the way."

"Yeah," said Glover. "That makes sense. Well, what are you going to do?"

"Nothing."

"Nothing?"

"I'll wait for him to make a move. Like I said, he might just be passing through."

Glover lifted his coffee cup but did not sip. He held it up and stared into it for a moment in silence. "But, Slocum," he said, "if, like you say, this Marley is a professional killer, one who's never missed, then you—"

"I'll be all right, Larry," said Slocum. "Don't worry."

"Should I tell June?"

"Not just yet."

"Damn it," Glover snarled. "I wish I knew who was behind all this."

"I'm beginning to get an idea, Larry," said Slocum. "I wish I could figure out the why of it."

It was early in the afternoon when Broderick Marley walked into Glover's store. He stepped in quietly and stood for a moment looking the place over. Glover was off to one side straightening some merchandise on a shelf. June had taken a break and gone for coffee. Millie was behind the counter. Slocum was sitting in a chair against the far wall. At the sight of Marley, he stood, ready for anything. Marley walked slowly across the room to the counter.

"Yes, sir?" said Millie.

"I need a box of forty-five shells," Marley said in a quiet, smooth voice.

Millie turned to get the bullets. She placed them on the counter and Marley paid her. She gave him some change, and he picked up the box and dropped it in a coat pocket. "Will there be anything else?" Millie asked.

"No," said Marley. "Not unless you'd like to go for a ride with me when you get off work. You're a right pretty little thing, miss."

"Well, I—n-no, thank you," Millie stammered. "I don't even know you."

"My name is Broderick Marley, miss. And you're—"

"Millie," she said.

"Well, maybe next time," he said. "Now that we've been introduced."

He turned, gave Slocum a deliberate look, then walked back out the door as slowly and deliberately as he had come in. Glover hurried over to the counter. "Millie," he said, "you handled that just right, but watch out for that man."

"What's wrong?" she asked.

"He's a killer. A professional. I suspect that he's been brought in here by whoever it is trying to ruin us."

"He did give me a kind of a cold chill," Millie said.

"For good reason," said Glover. "Till he's gone, we won't leave you alone in here."

"Oh, I'll be all right," said Millie, trying to shrug off the incident. "I can handle myself."

"Just the same," said Glover, "we won't leave you alone."

Millie glanced over at Slocum. "He's right," said Slocum. "I don't think Marley will try anything stupid, but watch out for him anyhow."

"Do you know him?" Millie asked Slocum.

"Only by reputation."

Toward evening, Slocum made his way over to the Whistle Stop. He made a point to not appear as if he was looking for anyone, but he saw Marley sitting alone at a far table, drinking coffee. Slocum stopped at the bar and ordered a shot of whiskey. He drank it down and ordered another. With his second drink, he found an unoccupied table and sat down. In a few minutes, Marley came walking over, carrying his cup of coffee. He stopped at Slocum's table and stood looking down at Slocum. Slocum returned the man's stare.

"Mind if I join you?" Marley said.

Slocum waited a moment, then shrugged and said, "Suit yourself."

Marley pulled out a chair and sat. "My name's Broderick Marley."

"I know," said Slocum.

"And you're John Slocum."

"I know that, too."

"I've heard of you, Slocum. I sure as hell never thought that I'd find you clerking in a store, though."

"It's honest work," Slocum said.

"Do you know who I am?"

"I know who you are, and I know what you are," Slocum said.

"What have you heard about me?"

"I've heard that you're a cold-blooded bastard who'll kill anything for a price."

"I don't kill women and children," Marley said. "When a man gets a reputation, it gets built up some with lies."

"That so?"

Slocum sipped his drink.

"Slocum, I've been around for a while. I've never had a bullet in me, and I've finished every job I ever took."

"Are you trying to impress me?"

"I guess I am. You see, Slocum, I'm being paid to get rid of you. It don't matter to me or to the man who's paying me whether I kill you or run you out of town, so if you were to just pack up and ride out, I'd forget the whole thing."

"Just like that?"

"Just like that. I get the same money either way. There's no need for you to die here."

"All men die, Marley," Slocum said. He finished his drink and held up the glass. The bartender saw it and brought the bottle. "Leave it," said Slocum. He told himself that he had better be careful. This was not the time to get drunk. Marley was sober as a judge, and it looked like he intended to stay that way.

"We all got to die someday, Slocum," said Marley. "That's for sure, but there's no reason for you to hurry that day up. I'll give you till morning to make up your mind."

"Forget it," said Slocum. "I can't think of a damn place I want to go to."

Marley shrugged. "I gave you fair warning," he said.

"Yeah. I guess I ought to appreciate that. Marley, let me ask you a question."

"Go on and ask."

"Who is it that's paying you for this job?"

Marley grinned. "I never tell, Slocum. You ought to know that."

"Yeah. Well, it just seems to me that someone's going to an awful lot of trouble and expense to run a storekeeper out of business."

"Is that how you see it?"

"That's the only way to look at it."

Slocum poured himself another drink. Marley motioned for a refill of coffee, and the bartender brought it in a hurry.

"You know, Slocum," said Marley, "I could like you. If we'd met under different circumstances—"

"I'd still say that you were a cold-blooded bastard," said Slocum.

Marley laughed. "God damn it, Slocum," he said, "I do like you. There ain't many men who would talk to me like that, especially when they're trying to get themselves drunk."

"I don't have anything to worry about," said Slocum. "You already told me that you'll give me till morning to make up my mind."

"Hell, I might give you longer than that."

"You'll have to shoot me in the back," Slocum said.

"You that good?" said Marley, with a smile.

"No," said Slocum. "I ain't, but I won't draw on you, and I've heard that you're a real careful man. There are no dodgers out on you. I've already checked that out."

"Oh, I'll get to you, Slocum. Make no mistake. I'll get to you, one way or another."

"So you'll gun me down, get paid off, and ride off to the next job?"

"No. This is much bigger than that. Hell, Slocum, you're going to be my retirement."

Marley picked up his cup and stood. "It's been nice visiting with you," he said. "Till next time." He walked back over to the table he had abandoned and sat down again, still looking at Slocum, and still smiling. Slocum finished his drink and left the Whistle Stop. He walked back over to the store and was surprised to see the lights still on in the place. He paused, pulled out his Colt, thumbed back the hammer and eased his way to the door. He looked sideways through the window, and then he saw Larry Glover sitting at a table working with his books. He put away his revolver and walked in.

"Larry," he said, "what are you doing here this time of night?"

"Oh, hi, Slocum," said Glover. "I just had some book-keeping I had to catch up with. That's all. Are you fixing to turn in? I'll be out of your hair in just a few minutes."

"No. Hell. That don't make any difference."

"You're acting a little jumpy."

"I just had a long visit with Broderick Marley," Slocum said. "He told me he's here to kill me."

Glover put down his pencil and stood up, a concerned expression on his face. "He just up and told you that?"

"Well, not just like that," said Slocum. "We visited for a while. I asked him who hired him, but he wouldn't say. I didn't expect him to."

"But he actually said that he intends to kill you?"

"Well, he did give me a choice. He said I could ride out of here in the morning. He gets paid the same, whether he kills me or runs me off."

"Slocum, me and June, we appreciate everything you've done for us, but I think it's time you went on. There's no sense in you going up against a man like that for us. It's not your problem."

"I'm not going anywhere, Larry."

"What if I fire you?"

"I'll still stay. I'm not going to be run off."

"But, Slocum—"

"Larry, I told you how the man works. I just won't draw on him. That's all. He'll have to try to ambush me or something, and I'll be real careful."

"Well, god damn it," said Glover. "You'd better be."

"Hell, Larry, he even told me he likes me."

18

Marley stepped out of the Whistle Stop the next day at just the time Thad Slater was pulling up in front of the hotel in a buggy. Marley watched as young Slater stepped down out of the buggy and walked around to meet Millie, who had just stepped out onto the sidewalk with a picnic basket on her arm. Slater tipped his hat and took the basket, which he placed in the buggy. Then he took Millie's hand. He walked her to the buggy and helped her up into the seat. Marley walked toward the buggy. With Millie seated, Thad walked around to the other side to climb back onto the seat. He was just about to flick the reins, when Marley stopped close by. Marley touched the brim of his hat politely.

"Good morning," he said.

"Good morning," said Millie, a little nervousness betraying itself in her voice.

"I wasn't spying on you, ma'am," Marley said. "I just stepped out the door over yonder when I seen the buggy pull up for you. I want to apologize for my forwardness of yesterday. I had no idea that you already had yourself a beau. I hope that you'll forgive me."

"That's quite all right, Mr. Marley," Millie answered. "There was certainly no harm done. May I present Mr. Thad Slater? Thad, this is Mr. Marley."

"How do you do?" said Thad.

"It's a pleasure, Mr. Slater," said Marley. He tipped his

hat again and turned to walk away. Thad flicked the reins, and the buggy pulled away with a lurch. Marley walked over to the eating place. Inside, he found himself a table and ordered coffee and a breakfast. Just then, Slocum came walking in. "Slocum," called Marley. "Would you care to join me?"

Slocum walked over to the table where Marley was sitting. He stood for a moment looking down at the gunfighter. "I'll buy your breakfast," said Marley.

Slocum pulled out a chair and sat down. "Why so generous? Last meal or something like that?" he asked.

Marley smiled. "I like you, Slocum," he said. "Till the time comes, we might as well be friends. Don't you think?"

"I suppose it don't matter if I get killed by a friend or an enemy," Slocum said. "But I haven't exactly taken a special liking to you. Not yet."

"I grow on you," said Marley. The waiter came with more coffee and took Slocum's order, then disappeared again.

"Do you get paid a fee plus expenses," Slocum asked, "or just a flat fee?"

"What makes you ask that?" said Marley.

"Oh, I was just wondering if this breakfast is coming out of your own pocket or if it's part of your expenses. That's all."

Marley chuckled. "I get expenses," he said.

"Are you thinking that you can do something over breakfast to make me mad enough to fight you?"

"Naw, I know it won't be that easy," Marley said. "You may not believe it, but I think I know you pretty well."

"You just met me," said Slocum.

"You're like an open book, Slocum. You've got honor and integrity and a whole lot of patience."

"You might have read me wrong," Slocum said. He picked up his coffee cup and took a sip. The coffee was strong and tasted good. "I might be the kind that would shoot you in the back."

"I don't think so," said Marley.

"You better be sure," said Slocum. "You could be betting your life on it."

"I'm pretty sure that I'm doing just that, but I also only bet on sure things."

The waiter came back with their breakfasts and left them on the table. Marley set to with no further nonsense. Slocum watched him for a moment, and then he did the same. *Might as well let the son of a bitch buy my breakfast,* he thought. Then he saw Larry and June Glover come walking in. He noticed that they each gave him a peculiar look. Well, he would tell them about it later. They took a table across the room. Patton came in next. He was alone. He walked by the table where the two enemies sat together.

"Good morning, Mr. Marley," he said. "Slocum."

Patton then walked over to join the Glovers. Slocum saw him speaking to the Glovers in low tones and occasionally looking over his shoulder at Marley and Slocum eating together. Slocum wondered what Patton might be saying, but he dismissed it as unimportant. Marley had one more cup of coffee after he had finished his breakfast. Then he stood up.

"Till next time, Slocum," he said. "I'll take care of your bill."

Slocum nodded at Marley and watched him leave the place. He finished his breakfast, had another cup of coffee and got up to leave. As he walked close by the table with the Glovers and Patton, Larry Glover called out to him. "Slocum." Slocum turned his head.

"I'll see you over at the store," Slocum said.

Patton watched Slocum walk out, and then he said, "That was mighty peculiar, don't you think?"

"Well," said June, "it does make me curious."

"That's all?" said Patton.

"What are you getting at, Pat?" asked Larry.

"Well, nothing, I guess. Maybe I should mind my own business, but that man is a gunfighter, don't you know? And all of your trouble started when Slocum came into town, didn't it? Then there were the two of them sitting together. Eating. What does that all add up to?"

"Nothing," said June. "Slocum has done nothing but help us, Pat. So I don't want to hear anything against him."

"Suit yourself," Patton said. "It's not my store."

When the Glovers got over to their store, they found it already open. Slocum was there. "Slocum," said Larry. "I want to talk to you."

June gave Larry a hard look. "Larry," she said, "don't say anything stupid."

"Don't worry," he said.

Slocum stepped out from behind the counter. "What is it, Larry?" he asked.

"What were you doing with that gunslinger?"

"Larry," said June sharply.

"It's all right, June," said Slocum. "I reckon he's got a right to ask."

"You're damn right I do," said Larry.

"He was there when I walked in," Slocum said. "He called out to me and invited me to sit with him. I was curious about what he had on his mind, so I sat down."

"That's it?"

"That's it."

"What did he have on his mind?"

"Killing me, I reckon."

"Did he say as much?"

"He'd already told me that last night in the bar," said Slocum. "This morning, he told me he liked me. Wanted to buy my breakfast. I figure he's just trying to set me up where he can catch me off guard."

"Well," said Larry, "it just seems mighty peculiar. That's all."

"Professional killers are a peculiar bunch," said Slocum. "Don't ever be surprised at anything they might say or do."

"Tell me, Slocum, are you a professional?

"I've had to hire my gun out a time or two," Slocum said.

"Yeah?" said Larry. "Well, I been wondering, how come my trouble started at just the time you hit town?"

"Larry," said June.

"I can't answer that one, Larry," Slocum said. "If I could answer it for you I would."

"Larry, we should be thankful that Slocum came to town when he did. He's—"

"And all the trouble at the store has happened when you were here. There were no other witnesses."

"That's not true, Larry," June said. "Slocum wasn't here when—"

"Now that gunfighter's buying you breakfast. You two looked pretty chummy over there together."

Slocum picked up his hat and pulled it on. "Larry, I'll get out of here if that's what you want," he said.

"Slocum," said June, "don't listen to him. He's just upset."

"I'm sorry, June," said Slocum. "I won't be questioned like a criminal."

Slocum walked out the door and shut it behind him. June started to follow him but thought better of it. She turned to Larry with a fury. "Now you've done it," she said.

"Done what?"

"You've run off the only friend we've had. You've left us alone in this fight. Now how are you going to deal with it?"

"I know who my friends are," said Larry.

"I don't think you do."

"We haven't had any trouble for a while anyhow," said Larry. "Maybe it's all behind us."

"I doubt that."

"Anyhow, maybe I'll sell out to Patton."

June stomped out of the store, and Larry sat down heavily in a chair at the end of the counter. He put an elbow on the counter, his head in his hand. "Oh, hell," he said, "what have I done?"

Slocum was headed for the hotel as June came running up behind him. He stopped when he became aware of her approach.

"Slocum," she said. "I'm sorry about Larry. I guess the

strain has just been too much for him. And then this morning, Pat Patton said all those things that Larry was saying to you. I didn't believe they had gotten to him, but I guess they did."

"Patton, huh?" said Slocum. "I kind of figured that."

"Slocum, please—"

"June," said Slocum, "don't worry. I'm fixing to get myself a room in here. I'll be over to the store for my things in a little while. As far as Larry knows, I'm through. But I'll still be here, June. And I'll be watching. I don't want you to worry none. Larry will come around."

"I just don't know what to say."

Slocum smiled at her. "Then don't say anything, June," he said. "Now go on back to the store, and don't blame Larry too much. Like you said, it's the strain he's been under. You know, having a lovely wife to support with a business like that—that takes a lot of courage just under normal circumstances. And Larry's circumstances here lately ain't been none too normal. Try to relax. Okay?"

June hesitated a moment. Then she said, "Okay, Slocum. I'll try."

"And when you get back over there, don't fuss at him. Don't even mention this little episode again. It'll all pass."

June walked slowly back toward the store as Slocum went into the hotel and got himself a room. He pocketed the key and walked out again. Standing there on the street, he contemplated his next move. He was thinking of Pat Patton. Just then, he saw Patricia come walking along the street. What a coincidence, he thought. He stepped out in her path to block her way.

"Good morning, Patricia," he said.

"Oh. Good morning, Slocum."

"I missed you at breakfast," he said.

"Oh, I just slept late this morning," she said. "I just had to."

"Have you had your breakfast?"

"Well, no."

"May I accompany you?"

"Sure," she said with a broad smile.

Slocum walked along with Patricia to the eating place,

and they went inside. She ordered a breakfast, and he ordered coffee. There were only a few customers in the place, as it was getting late in the morning.

"You're looking awful pretty this morning," said Slocum.

"Thank you," she said.

"It seems a shame to me," he said. "A pretty girl like you stuck in a place like this. Oh, I'd think it was just fine if I meant to hang around. I'd be just tickled to have you nearby. But I never stay around one place too long. I sure hate to think about you being stuck here with no one but a bunch of no-good cowhands and—"

"Oh, don't worry about me, Slocum," she said. "I won't be around here much longer." She gave Slocum a knowing look.

"You won't?" he said.

"You can bet your life on that," she said. "We'll be moving out of here. Real soon. Probably to San Francisco. Have you ever been to San Francisco?"

"Yeah. I been there."

"Tell me about it, Slocum."

"Well, what can I tell you? It's a big city all right. It's got everything a place needs to make a girl happy. Lots of swank places to eat. Lots of handsome young men in suits and ties driving fancy carriages around all over the place. You'll like it there, and you'll feel right at home, too."

"You really think I'll fit in?"

"Oh, hell," said Slocum, "there ain't no question about that. They got lots of pretty girls, but I never seen any as pretty as you are. Why, you get out there and buy you some new clothes in one of them fancy San Francisco shops and—"

"What's wrong with my clothes?" she said, interrupting him.

"There ain't nothing wrong with your clothes," he said. "Only out there, they got all the latest in women's fashions, you know. They come in on the big ships from all around the world. You'll look just great in one of them dresses straight from Paris."

"Paris?"

"Yeah. That's in France, you know. You'll be the most fanciest woman in San Francisco and you'll have all the young men on your doorstep, too. Why, they'll be fighting over you. I bet you'll have yourself a rich young husband in just no time."

"Oh, God," she said, "I can hardly wait."

"Just what is it you're waiting for?" he asked.

"Well," she said, "don't say anything. Okay?"

"Oh, no," said Slocum. "I'll keep just as quiet as can be about it."

"Well, Daddy's got some kind of big business deal in the works," she said, "and when it goes through, we'll be all set up. Then he'll sell out the Whistle Stop, and we'll be on our way."

"Well, I'll be damned," said Slocum. "You don't say?"

19

Thad Slater drove the buggy back toward his father's ranch. Neither he nor Millie said anything about the direction he was going. They made small talk about the weather. It was a very nice day. They talked about the stranger in town. Yes, indeed, he was a rather mysterious man, but polite. Millie told Thad about the way in which Marley had approached her, and then they both opined as how it was very gracious of Mr. Marley to offer an apology when he had seen Thad picking her up that morning.

"When he said that I had a beau," Millie said, "I didn't correct him. I hope you didn't mind too much"

"Oh, no," said Thad. "I didn't mind. In fact, I was kind of hoping that you meant it. For real."

Millie looked down without responding, but she had a smile on her face. The buggy approached the main gate to the Slater ranch, but Thad drove right on past it.

"Where are we going, Thad?" Millie questioned.

"Oh, nowhere in particular," said Thad. "Just for a ride. That's all. Is anything wrong?"

She grabbed his arm with both of hers and hugged it to her. "No," she said. "Of course not."

"There's a very nice spot up here a ways I'd like to show you," Thad said. "It will probably be near time to eat lunch by the time we get there."

"All right," she said.

The road carried them up into the mountains, and when

Thad pulled the buggy off to one side of the road, Millie discovered that they were just on the edge of a mountain, with a spectacular view of the broad valley below.

"Oh," she said, "it's beautiful."

Thad got down, walked around and helped Millie out of the buggy. She walked toward the edge, but she stopped before she got too close for comfort. Thad stepped up beside her and put an arm around her shoulders.

"It is, isn't it?" he said.

"Is it still your ranch?" she asked.

"It's Dad's way over to the other side of the valley there," he said, pointing. Mountains rose up again on the far side. Down in the valley, cattle could be seen contentedly grazing.

"Your cattle?" Millie asked.

"Yeah. Well, Dad's."

"But they're yours, too, aren't they?"

"Well, I suppose so. In a way. That is, they will be one of these days, if I live long enough."

"What a terrible thing to say."

He laughed. "Well, of course, I expect to," he said.

Just then, Millie turned her head to look up into Thad's face. He returned the gaze, and they stared at one another for a long moment in silence. She turned to face him, reaching up to put both hands on his shoulders. He leaned forward, and their lips met in a long and luxurious kiss. At last they broke apart, and Thad said, in a rather embarrassed voice, "Are you hungry? I am."

"I'll get the lunch," said Millie, and she walked back to the buggy for the basket. Thad got a blanket out of the buggy and spread it out on the ground. They sat down, and Millie opened up the basket.

Back in Mesa Poquita, Slocum walked into the Glovers' store. Larry looked up from his work with a solemn expression on his face. He opened his mouth as if to speak, but Slocum spoke first.

"I'll just be getting my things out of the back room," he said.

"Slocum," said Larry. Slocum paused and looked at Larry, and Larry said only, "All right. Go ahead."

As Slocum walked past the counter, June looked at him. She looked as if she wanted to say something, too, but Slocum shushed her with a reassuring look. He went on into the back room.

At the livery stable, Broderick Marley rode out on his big black horse. As he rode out of town, he was headed in the direction of the Slater ranch. He rode calmly, casually. The expression on his face could not be read.

Millie and Thad finished their lunch and packed up the basket and the blanket in the buggy. Their picnic place looked untouched as they climbed back into the buggy to leave. Thad kept driving in the same direction they had been going. Not back toward town. In another few minutes, they came to a small cabin. Thad stopped.

"This is the end of our ranch here," he said. "This is an old line cabin of ours. It's not in use just now."

"Can we get out and look at it?" asked Millie.

"Sure," said Thad, and his heart was pounding. He drove the buggy right up to the front of the cabin, got out and tied the horses, then walked over to help Millie down out of the buggy. Holding her hand, he led her to the front door and opened it. The light inside was dim. The cabin was neat, but the furniture was covered with a layer of dust.

"It's only used at roundup time," Thad said. "It's been a few months now. I'm afraid it needs a cleaning."

Millie looked over at the bed, then back at Thad. She pulled him toward the bed. "It'll do just fine," she said. Standing beside the bed, she turned her back to him and said, "Can you undo me?"

Thad fumbled with the hooks on the back of the dress, but eventually he got them undone. Millie turned back to face him as she started to slither out of the dress. Thad took off his hat and spun it aside. They undressed quickly, as if they were running out of time. Naked, Thad reached for the blanket that covered the bed. He grabbed it by a corner and ripped it aside, and the dust flew. Millie sat on the edge of the bed looking up at him. She picked up her feet and scooted her naked ass over to make room for him. He climbed in beside her, breathing hard, his rod already standing erect, and he reached for her with both arms. They embraced and they kissed.

Thad's trembling hand groped for a breast and, finding it, kneaded it like dough. Millie moaned through the kiss and parted her lips to make an opening for his probing tongue. Tongues still dueling, his hand slipped from her breast and roamed down her smooth belly until it found her hairy mound. There it hesitated, pressed the firm, soft flesh beneath the hair.

"Oh," said Thad.

"Um," said Millie.

Thad began feeling around with his finger until he had located the inviting slit. His finger fought its way inside and then roamed up and down. At last it found the lovely hole in there, and it poked its way all the way inside, slipping in the slimy juices that now flowed freely. The walls of her healthy young snatch gripped and released his finger repeatedly. Thad slipped his finger back out of the hole and slid it toward the top of the slit, where it found the little nubbin waiting anxiously for attention. As he fingered it, Millie began to roll her hips and moan more loudly.

She reached down with both hands for his throbbing tool. One hand gripped it hard while the other began to fondle his now-heavy balls. "Oh, Thad," she said, "Thad. Put that in me. Put it all the way in."

Thad rolled over on top of her, wriggling his way between her wide-spread legs, and she guided the pulsing tool into her pleasure hole. As soon as he could feel that he was in the right place, Thad thrust forward. He slid comfortably all the way in, his entire length swallowed by her hungry cunt.

"Oh!" he said.

"Ah," said Millie. "Fuck me, Thad. Fuck me."

There was no building up to it now. That was long past. Thad began to hump fast and furiously, his balls slapping against her ass as his rod plunged in and out, and her juices ran down her thighs and onto the cheeks of her ass and finally pooled on the bed beneath them.

"Oh, oh, oh!"

"Ah, ah, ah!"

She slapped his ass hard with both hands, grabbing a cheek with each and digging her fingernails in.

"Ahhh," he cried, and he pumped even harder and faster. He was breathing hard and fast, and so was Millie. At last, desperate as he was, he had to stop to try to catch his breath. Millie decided to take advantage of the pause. She pushed him away.

"Wait. Wait," she said.

As Thad withdrew, Millie rolled over and raised herself onto her hands and knees. Thad, up on his knees, looked at the magnificent ass that was thrust toward him. He reached down to feel the soppy place between her upper thighs, and she said, "Now, Thad. Put it in me again."

He scooted up close to her behind, grasped his cock and pressed it toward her. She reached back between her legs to take hold of it again and guide it home, and Thad began humping furiously once more. Suddenly he felt a tremendous pressure building in his loins and screamed, "Ahhh!" He pumped faster and more desperately, and then came the explosion, the sudden release. It spurted again and again, and Millie felt the hot juices surging into her depths.

At last, Thad rested on knees behind her, panting for breath, his cock still embedded in her cunt, relaxing as he had never relaxed before. Slowly his huge erection wilted and slipped out of her pocket. Then he rolled over, falling onto his back beside her.

"Oh, Millie," he said. "That was—"

"Wonderful," she said.

"Yes. It was. Millie, I—"

She rolled over and leaned over his face to give him a kiss. Staying close to his face, she said, "What?"

"Millie," he said, "I hope you don't think I'm being too fast, but I . . . I love you."

"Oh, Thad," she said. "I love you, too."

"Millie, will you marry me?"

"Oh, yes," she said. "Of course I will."

"Let's do it right away," he said. "I don't want to wait."

"We'll have to tell your father."

"We'll go right now to tell him."

"Yes," she said. "All right."

She kissed him again, and then she began slowly tonguing her way down his stomach. He gasped for breath. Within a couple of inches of his now-limp member, she smiled up at him and began to slowly tickle his balls. "Oh," he moaned. She leaned forward and kissed the head of the now-harmless monster. Then she lifted it up and studied it. Finally, she took the head into her mouth, and Thad thought that he would die right then and there. He found that there was life yet in his tool, as it began to grow and harden again inside her warm mouth. Then she began to slurp and to move her head up and down along the length of his shaft.

Soon Thad was humping again, thrusting his hips and his rod upward as Millie's head descended. Faster and faster she moved, and his own thrusting kept pace with her. He felt the buildup in his loins again. He felt the pressure increasing. He knew that he was about to explode once more. He felt helpless in her grasp, and he loved it. He pumped harder and harder, and then he felt the first shot burst into her mouth, and the second, and the third. At last, he lay still again, and she was back beside him, kissing his lips and his chest.

"Do you still love me?" she said.

"I love you more than ever," he said.

"Then let's get up and get dressed and go see your father."

"Yes," he said, jumping out of the bed. "Yes. Let's do that."

Marley rode along, casually following the tracks of the buggy. He came to the spot where the buggy had pulled off to the side of the road, and he paused for a moment. He figured they had stopped there for a spell. Then he continued following the tracks. Soon he found himself at the top of a rise looking down on a small cabin. The buggy was parked in front. He smiled. He moved his horse into the trees out of sight, and he dismounted, taking the rifle from the scabbard. Placing himself behind a convenient tree, he cranked a shell into the chamber and waited.

In another few minutes, the door opened and Millie stepped out, followed by Thad. Thad closed the door and escorted Millie to the buggy, where he kissed her tenderly, then helped her up onto the seat. Then he untied the horses. He walked around to the other side of the buggy and climbed up, taking the reins. He looked at Millie, and she looked up at him. Skillfully, he backed the rig up, then he turned it up onto the road, snapping the buggy whip.

Up on the hillside from his hiding place, Marley raised his rifle slowly and took careful aim. He squeezed the trigger, and a bullet spanged into the side of the cabin. Millie screamed and Thad pulled out his six-gun and looked around desperately. "Get down, Millie," he said, jumping out of the buggy and still looking around. Millie scrunched down in the buggy, in front of the seat. Nothing more happened. Quickly, Thad mounted the buggy again and took up the reins, aiming the rig for the road. Then there was a second shot, which kicked up dirt in front of the horses' hooves. The horses neighed and reared, and Thad fought them with the reins. He managed to get them moving along the road. He lashed at them, but the lashing was unnecessary. The horses were already running desperately for fear back toward the main gate of the ranch.

Marley, still smiling, sent a final shot after them, and he laughed softly as they raced desperately away. He had no desire to hurt the two young people. He would not be paid for that. But he had an idea that if he frightened them badly enough, Slocum would come after him. And it was Slocum he wanted. Like he had said to Slocum, there were ways of getting to him. He figured this was one way. He would give the buggy a good head start, and then he would ride back into town. He would wait for a reaction from Slocum.

20

Old Sam Slater was sitting in his easy chair sipping a cup of coffee and smoking a long cigar when he heard the sounds of the buggy racing toward his house. He put down the cup and got up from his chair as quickly as he could. Walking to the door, he grabbed up the rifle that stood beside it, then jerked open the door and went out onto the porch. He saw that the buggy was driven by his son, and that Thad had a female passenger. He had known that Thad was going to take Millie for a drive. He put down the rifle, leaning it against the wall, and he walked to the edge of the porch. Very close to the porch, Thad brought the buggy to a halt.

"Thad," said Slater. "What the hell are you driving like that for?"

"Dad," his son said "someone out on the road took some shots at us."

"What?" said the old man. He looked toward the corral, where he saw two cowhands, and he hollered at them. They started toward the house. Then back to Thad and Millie, he said, "You two get in the house." As Thad got himself out of the buggy and was helping Millie down, the two cowboys came up to the porch. Old Slater told one of them to take care of the buggy and the other to get a rifle and keep his eyes on the road. Then he followed Thad and Millie into the house. He poured two glasses of brandy and gave them to Thad and Millie. He paused for a second, then went back and poured another one for himself. They all three sat down.

"All right now," said old Slater, "tell me about it."

There really wasn't much to tell, but Thad told his father about the ambusher up by the line shack. How he had fired three shots at them. They had all come close, but luckily they had all missed.

"Did he follow you?" asked Slater.

"Not that I could tell," said Thad.

"Oh, I was so frightened," said Millie.

"Well, you should've been," said Slater, "but it's all right now. You got any idea who it was?"

"No, sir," said Thad. "I sure ain't. I been trying to figure who it might have been, but I can't come up with no idea."

"I'll send a couple of the boys out to track," Slater said. "I doubt if they can come up with anything, but it's something to try."

"Yes, sir."

"Mr. Slater?" said Millie.

"What is it?" he answered.

"I been thinking, too," she said, "and the only thing that comes to my mind is that someone's been after the Glovers, you know, and I been working for the Glovers."

"You mean the shooter might have been after you?" said Thad.

"I reckon it could be," said Millie. "I'm sorry if I got you into this. You know that Mr. Marley? Well, Mr. Slocum thinks that he might be here working for them that's after the Glovers. And he seen us ride out of town this morning."

"That's right, Dad," Thad said.

"Well, we can't go gunning a man for suspicion," said Slater, "but we sure can go investigating." He headed for the door.

"Where you going, Dad?"

"I'm fixing to set on my trackers and to have me a horse saddled up," the old man said. "I'll get you one, too. Little lady, you can stay right here till we get back."

"Oh, I don't want to—"

"Nonsense," said Slater. "You won't be in no one's way." He went on out the door without another word.

"It's best, Millie," said Thad. "Dad's going to want me to ride along with him, and I sure don't want you riding back to town by yourself. We'll get you back all right later. Okay?"

"Okay, Thad. Thad?"

"What?"

"Do you think that this is the time to tell him—I mean, about us?"

"I don't see why not."

"Well, because it might seem like this is all because of me," she said.

"Nonsense."

Just then old Slater came back into the house, and Thad stood up to face him.

"Dad," he said, "there's something else."

"Well, shoot," said the old man.

"Me and Millie, we're fixing to get married—just as soon as possible."

Old Slater looked from his son to Millie, and he smiled. "Well now," he said, "that's just great. All the more reason for you to stay here, little lady, while we go chasing around looking for owlhoots. There'll be a better time for saying things to one another. Right now, we got work to do."

Thad kissed Millie before going out of the house, and Millie said, "Thad, be careful."

"Don't worry," he said. "I will."

Slocum was lounging in front of the hotel when he saw Marley walking from the livery stable back toward the Whistle Stop. He didn't think too much about it. He couldn't think of anything that Marley could have been up to so early in the morning, and besides, he had his eye on the Glovers' store. Everything was all right there. He thought about following Marley into the bar for a drink, but he decided against it. He leaned back in his chair against the front wall of the hotel and pulled out a cigar from his pocket. He got a match, struck it and lit the cigar.

The cigar was about smoked up when he saw old Slater and Thad, with a couple of cowhands, ride into town.

He stood up and walked to meet them. They pulled up their horses in the middle of the street. "What's up, Slater?" he asked. Then he looked at Thad. "Where's Millie?"

"Millie's out at the ranch house, Slocum," said Thad. "She's all right, but listen—"

"She rode out of here with you in a buggy," Slocum said. "Now you come riding back on a horse without her. That worries me a little."

"I can explain all that," said Thad.

"I'm listening."

"This ain't no place for explanations," said the old man. "Let's go inside someplace."

They wound up inside the eating place, which was almost devoid of customers. They ordered coffee and sat at a table in a corner.

"All right," said Slocum. "I'm waiting."

Thad told Slocum of his ride with Millie, the picnic and the shooting outside the line shack. He omitted the part about what had gone on inside the shack. He did tell Slocum that Millie had agreed to marry him. He also told Slocum about Millie's suspicions, that whoever it was who was behind the attacks on the Glovers was also behind the shootings.

Slocum took a sip of his coffee. He thought for a moment in silence. Impatient, old Slater said, "I sent out some men to try to track the shooter, and we come in here to check up on that black-suited son of a bitch."

"Well, hold on a minute there," Slocum said. "Millie's suspicions make sense, but let's just think about it for a bit. I doubt if your men can find any tracks that will be helpful. And if Marley was the shooter, which he likely was, then he wasn't aiming to kill anyone. He was just trying to scare you, and the reason he was doing that was to try to get to me. I'm the one he means to kill."

All of a sudden, Slocum felt like he could take the Slaters into his confidence, and he told them of his two talks with Broderick Marley. He also told them about Patton's comments to Glover and how Glover had reacted, and he finished off by telling them what Patricia had said about moving to San Francisco.

"All we need is some proof," he said.

"What more proof do you need than what you've just told us?" said Slater.

"I need some proof that Patton hired Marley," Slocum said. "It's too late to look for proof that he hired all them others. They're dead and gone."

"How're you going to get that?" Thad asked.

"I ain't sure. Just by watching Marley, I guess," Slocum said. "Say, when's the wedding?"

Thad looked at his father and then back at Slocum. "We, uh, haven't had time to figure that out," he said. "If I had my way, it would be today."

"Let's make it next week," said the old man. "That'll give us time to announce it and invite some folks out to the ranch. We'll make a big party out of it."

"All right, Dad."

"That sounds great," said Slocum. "And since it's all arranged, why don't you all just keep Millie out there from now on? I'll tell June Glover that she won't be back to work."

"All right," said Slater, "and thanks."

"You all go back to the ranch now," Slocum said. "Keep your eyes and ears open, but don't start anything. Okay?"

"All right," said old Slater. "Whatever you say. For now."

When the Slaters rode out of town, Slocum watched the store until he saw Larry leave. He hurried over to see June and tell her the news about Millie. June was genuinely pleased for Millie. Then he told her all of his latest appraisal of the situation, his suspicions of Marley and of Patton.

"So Pat's behind it all," she said.

"It sure looks that way to me," Slocum said. "We'll have to wait and watch a little more to be sure."

"Slocum, I—"

"Hey," he said, "there'll be time enough for that later.

Right now, I got to get out of here before Larry comes back. Don't worry. I'll be seeing you."

He walked out of the store and straight over to the saloon. He went up to the bar and ordered a bottle and two glasses. He paid for it and headed over to a table against the far wall where Marley was sitting with a cup of coffee. He put the bottle and the glasses down on the table, pulled out a chair and sat.

"I don't remember inviting you over," said Marley.

"But you said you liked me," said Slocum. "I didn't figure you'd mind."

"Why two glasses?"

"I thought I'd buy you a drink, Marley. You bought my breakfast. You can't hardly refuse me, now, can you?"

"I don't drink when I'm on the job," Marley said.

"You ain't on the job tonight," said Slocum. He poured two glasses of whiskey and shoved one toward Marley. "You done told me that your job is to kill me. You ain't going to kill me tonight. I know that, 'cause I ain't going to fight you tonight. Here. Have a drink with me."

Marley looked at the glass and said nothing.

"What's the matter, Marley? You can't think that I'd try to get you drunk and then pick a fight? I don't work like that."

Marley reached for the glass, picked it up and drained it in one gulp.

"There," he said. "Now perhaps you'll leave me alone."

Slocum drained his own glass and then refilled both. "We ain't finished," he said. "I figure you think I'll come gunning for you when I find out that you took some pot-shots at a couple of kids today." Marley looked up sharply. "Well, I know about that, and I also know that you wasn't aiming to hit them. Just scare them a bit. And maybe make me mad enough to come gunning for you."

Marley picked up the glass and took a sip.

"But you're not mad?" he asked.

"I ain't that mad," Slocum said. "Like I said, all you did was scare a couple of kids. They're all right."

"They might not be the next time."

"Oh, I don't think you'll bother them again." Slocum

sipped at his own second drink. "I've just been trying to figure out who it was that brought you in here."

"Any luck?"

"I've been eliminating people one at a time. I just have one left. It's got to be him. The only thing I can't figure out is how come."

"You got a hell of a lot of figuring to do, Slocum. I figure I'll have to kill you before you get it all figured out."

"Well, you might, but I kind of doubt it. You see, I figure that it was Pat Patton who hired you."

Marley took another sip of whiskey while Slocum tried to read his face. "Is that what you figure?" he said.

"Yeah," said Slocum. "For some reason, which I ain't yet figured, Patton wants the Glovers out of business. He tried using some common toughs, but they all got knocked out of the way. So he got desperate enough to cough up the bucks to bring you on. The reason he got you was so you could kill me and he could go on back to his old way of harassing the Glovers. Am I right so far?"

"You're telling this," said Marley. "I'm just listening."

"You're staying here at the Whistle Stop instead of over at the hotel," Slocum said. "That's a hint."

"This is the first place I stopped when I come to town," said Marley. "The man said he had a room, and he could provide a bath, too. I didn't see no reason to go no farther. That's all."

"Well, maybe," said Slocum.

"Slocum," said Marley, "you're on the wrong trail. Hell, I never even left town today."

"I saw you coming back from the livery," said Slocum.

"I just went down there to check on my horse. I'm very fond of my horse."

"Sure. Well, I've been wrong before," Slocum said, "but the main thing is that I ain't going to fight you till I get the answers to a couple of questions."

"Slocum," said Marley, "I'm changing my mind about you. I don't think I like you at all."

Slocum smiled at Marley and poured two more glasses of whiskey.

21

"But, Daddy," Patricia Patton was whining, "I can't stand it around this god-awful town for another day. Not one more day."

"Be patient, sweetie," said Patton. "It won't be long now. I promise you."

"But when?"

"Real soon, baby. Real soon."

"Daddy!"

"Look. I got a new man working on my deal. He'll get the job done in record time. We'll be out of here before you know it."

She stamped her feet and walked huffily across the room, turning back on him with a glare on her pretty young face. "I swear, Daddy, one more day and I'll be crazy. I might do something desperate if I have to stay around here for another day. The men are all old or they smell of cows. I'm going to be an old maid if I have to stay around here. I've got to get out, I tell you. I've got to."

Patton looked at his daughter, and he thought real hard. There would be advantages to having her out of the way, and he could follow her real soon. He had a friend with a fine hotel in San Francisco, and he had enough cash to send her on ahead. He also had a buyer already lined up for the Whistle Stop. He wasn't at all sure that he could take much more of her whining anyhow.

"All right, sweetheart," he said. He reached into his

pocket and pulled out a wad of bills, which he counted quickly and handed to her. She looked astonished, unbelieving. "Now, look," he said. "I have to stay here and wind up this business deal. You can understand that. This money will get you to San Francisco and tide you over till I join you. There's a stage out of here this afternoon for Denver. From there you can catch a train to San Francisco." He sat down at his desk and wrote out a name and address. Done with it, he handed it to his daughter. "When you get there," he said, "give this address to a cabbie, and when he leaves you at the hotel, ask for this man. He's a friend of mine. He'll see to it that you're well taken care of. All right? Is that what you want?"

Patricia sucked in a deep breath, threw open her arms and flung them around her father's neck. "Oh, Daddy," she said. "Daddy. I don't know what to say."

"Just get yourself packed," Patton said, "if you want to catch that stage this afternoon."

"I won't have to pack much," Patricia said. "When I get out there, I'll buy everything new."

Slocum was in the land office looking over the town plats. He found the location of the store all right, but he couldn't make anything out of it. Why the hell would Patton want that spot? Or if not that spot, why that store? None of it made any sense. He was pretty sure, from his observations, that Patton was raking in much more at the Whistle Stop than the Glovers were at their operation. He wished now that he had asked Larry just how much Patton had offered him for the store. He wasn't sure that information would help either. Still, he would like to know. Maybe he could catch June alone again before long. He thanked the man in the office and left. Standing on the sidewalk, he looked around, trying to figure a next move. He wanted to catch Patton talking to Marley. He really wanted to slip up on them and eavesdrop on their conversation. But he wasn't sure how to go about that. He knew already that Marley was sitting at his usual table in the Whistle Stop sipping coffee. He hoped that he had given the man enough whiskey the night before to cause him a hell of a hangover.

There was nothing else to do but watch the store. All was quiet over there. He decided to go back to his room in the hotel. From his window he had a good view of both the store and the Whistle Stop. That would be as good as, and less obvious than, watching from the street.

At about noon, Slocum saw Larry Glover go into the eating place. About fifteen minutes later, he watched as Broderick Marley came out of the Whistle Stop and walked to the eating place. In another twenty minutes, Larry came back out and headed back for the store. Slocum kept watching. He was getting hungry, but he wasn't yet ready to go out to eat. In another few minutes, Marley left, headed back for the Whistle Stop, and right after that Slocum saw June come out of the store. He decided that he would go eat. He left his room and walked downstairs. Then he went out of the hotel and across the street to the eating place. As he walked in, he acted surprised to see June.

"Sit down, Slocum," she said. She was alone at a table.

"Are you sure it's all right?" he asked.

"Larry's already had his lunch," she said. "With just the two of us in the store again, we have to eat in shifts. Please sit down."

Slocum pulled out a chair and sat. "You been doing all right?" he asked.

"Larry's been acting surly ever since you left—"

"You mean since he ran me off."

"Yes," she said. "Ever since then, but it's all right. Business is good. We haven't had any more trouble. Not yet."

"I hope you don't have," Slocum said.

June leaned across the table and spoke to Slocum in a low whisper. "Are you pretty sure then, that it's—"

Slocum shushed her with a finger over his lips. "I'm pretty damn sure, June," he said. "I need a break. That's all."

"What about that gunfighter?"

"I'll know when he's ready," Slocum said, "and I'll be ready for him."

As the waiter took their orders, Slocum studied June. She was a fine woman, still very much good-looking. In another outfit than that storekeeper's dress, she could be as ravishing as any other beautiful woman. Hell, she was anyway. Damn, he thought, if it wasn't for Larry . . .

They finished their meal and got up. Slocum stopped at the counter and paid for them. June protested, but he insisted. He walked with her out the door and halfway across the street, and they had to pause for a moment as the stage drew into town. June looked casually toward the stage as she started on her way into the store, but she stopped suddenly. "Excuse me," she said to Slocum, and she walked on over to the stage stop. Slocum stood watching her, and he noticed that Patricia was getting onto the stage. Her father was there seeing her off. June spoke to both of them briefly. Slocum waited as the stage pulled out and Patton headed back toward the Whistle Stop. June was moving again toward the store. Slocum headed her off.

"What was that all about?" he asked her.

"Pat said that he was sending Patricia to San Francisco."

Slocum hurried down to the livery stable and got his horse. He saddled it, mounted up and started at a lope after the stage. He rode easy for a while, letting the stage get a couple of miles out of town. Then he kicked his big Appaloosa into a run. "Let's catch it, boy," he said. Coming up close behind the stage, he pulled out his six-gun and fired a couple of shots into the air. He put the gun away again as the driver turned to look over his shoulder. Slocum pulled off his hat and waved. The stage kept rolling, and Slocum urged his big stallion on, riding up alongside the stage.

"Pull over," he called out to the driver.

"Is this a holdup?" the driver yelled.

"No, hell," said Slocum. "Pull over for a minute. I want to talk to one of your passengers. That's all."

The driver pulled up, and the stage rocked to a standstill. Slocum dismounted and opened the door. Patricia looked at him with surprise.

"Step out a minute," he said. "I came to tell you good-bye."

She allowed him to help her out of the stage, and he led her a few feet away from the earshot of the other passengers and the driver. "What is this?" said one of the passengers, and the driver shrugged.

"I heard you're headed for San Francisco," said Slocum.

"That's right," she said, a big smile spreading across her face. "I told you it wouldn't be long."

"You sure did," Slocum said, "but you were leaving without even telling me good-bye?"

"I'm sorry, but there just wasn't any time," she said. "I just talked Daddy into it this morning."

"And you're going out there all by yourself?"

"Daddy will be along real soon. He told me so. And he has a friend out there who has a nice hotel. That's where I'll be staying while I wait for him to come out. Slocum, the first thing I'm going to do—after I check into the hotel of course—is buy myself all new dresses."

"That's real nice, Patricia," Slocum said. "You say your daddy'll be right on out?"

"That's right."

"Does that mean that his business is all taken care of?"

"Hey," called the driver. "I've got a schedule to keep."

"What if I was to shoot one of your damn horses?" said Slocum. "What would that do to your schedule?"

The driver and the other passengers muttered to one another as Slocum turned back to Patricia.

"He said it would all be done real soon. He promised me. I think he may have a buyer for the Whistle Stop, and he's got a new man working for him on his other business. He said this new man is real good, and he'll get it all wrapped up in no time."

"Well, that's real nice," Slocum said. "I'm glad for you. Say, do you have an address where I can get in touch with you?"

"Why, yes," she said. She reached into her purse and pulled out the note her father had written for her. Fumbling around, she found another piece of paper and a pen-

cil, and she copied off the name and address and handed
it to Slocum.

"Thanks," he said. "Well, you better get back on the
stage. I think the driver's getting anxious."

"You're god damn right I am," the driver said.

Slocum helped Patricia back onto the coach, shut the
door and touched the brim of his hat. "You have fun out
there," he said.

"Oh, I will," said Patricia. "Don't you worry about
that."

The driver snapped the reins, and the horses took off.
The stage gave a lurch, jarring the passengers, and rolled
off down the road. Slocum stood there and watched it go,
thinking about the words that Patricia had said. So Patton
figured on having everything all wrapped up real soon.
That meant that Marley would have to act fast. He might
come after Slocum, or he might go after the store. If Patton was about to push him, there was no telling which
direction he might move. And if Marley really believed
that Slocum was no longer working for the Glovers, he
might think that his job was done where Slocum was concerned. He might just go straight for the store—or for the
Glovers. Slocum didn't like to think of that possibility.
He mounted up and turned the horse back toward town.

Slocum rode slow on his way back. It gave him time to
think, and he had a lot to think about. He still wanted to
find a way of spying on Patton and Marley together, but
so far as he knew, they had never even spoken together
alone. It had all been business—hotel business, that is,
and in front of the whole world. It looked like something
was about to happen, though, and he did not like to think
of Larry Glover trying to deal with it alone. Maybe he
would have to go back to Glover and try to explain to
him how things stood. But Glover wouldn't likely listen
to him. Slocum couldn't quite figure out what to do.

Back in town, he returned the Appaloosa to the stable
and walked back toward the hotel. Along the way, he saw
Larry Glover leaving the bank, on his way back to the store.
Slocum picked up his pace in order to intercept Glover.

"Hold up a minute, Larry," he said.

Glover stopped. "I didn't think you'd still be in town," he said.

"Why not?" said Slocum. "If you believe that I'm here to hurt you, why would I leave now?"

"On account of I found you out, I guess," said Glover.

"Damn it, Larry, you know that's a bunch of bullshit."

"I don't know any such thing. Get out of my way, Slocum."

Glover put a hand on Slocum's shoulder and shoved. Slocum reached up, grabbed the wrist, stepped back and threw Larry to the ground. Larry rolled over quickly and stood up, glaring at Slocum.

"Damn you, Slocum," he said.

"Hold on, Larry. You're no match for me."

"We'll see about that."

Larry rushed at Slocum and threw a roundhouse right. Slocum stepped aside, easily dodging the blow. Larry braced for another assault.

"Larry, don't," Slocum said.

Head down, Larry rushed Slocum, banging his head into Slocum's midsection and carrying them both to the ground. Slocum managed to wrestle Larry over, and then he stood up, leaving Larry on the ground.

"Stay there, Larry," Slocum said.

"You'd like that, wouldn't you?"

Larry got up again. He doubled his fists in front of his face and said, "Come on, you son of a bitch."

"Ah, hell," Slocum said. "Just forget it."

He started to walk away from Glover, but as he moved past him, Glover swung a right, catching Slocum just behind the ear. It was a hard blow, and it stung, and it made Slocum mad. He turned and drove a right into Larry's gut. Larry doubled over with a loud moan, and Slocum struck him a hard uppercut, which straightened him up. Then he popped him a left on the chin, knocking him over backwards. Larry wasn't out, but he didn't get up. He was on one elbow. His other hand rubbed his chin.

"It's just no use trying to talk to a stubborn jackass like you," Slocum said, and he walked on toward the hotel.

22

Larry stood up and staggered toward the store, and when he got close and looked up, there was June standing in the doorway with her hands on her hips looking at him very sternly. He paused a moment, then started walking again. When he reached the door, June did not move out of his way. He looked at her. She did not move. She did not speak. "What?" he said.

"What the hell have you been doing?" she snapped. "How did that get started?"

"Oh, hell," he said. "Never mind that."

He shoved his way past her and into the store, heading for the back room, so recently vacated by Slocum, and a pan of water he knew would be there on a table. June followed hard on his heels.

"Never mind!" she said. "Never mind! I damn well do mind. You've just been fighting in the street with the best friend we have, and I want to know what it was all about."

"Nothing," he said. "Just forget about it."

"You're just being stupid," she said. "Can't you see that?"

"You're the one that's blind," Larry said. He had been sloshing water on his face and now he reached for a towel. "Slocum's the cause of all this trouble."

"You know better than that," June said. She turned and stalked toward the front door. Larry took a few steps after her.

"Where the hell are you going?" he said.

"I'm going to see Slocum," she said. "And don't you try to stop me."

He thought of trying to respond, but something in her eyes made him keep his mouth shut. He stood there while June left the store. Then he went to the back room again, found a bottle of whiskey and poured himself a drink. He tossed it down all at once and then refilled the glass.

June had seen the direction Slocum was going when he left Larry in the street, so she followed him to his hotel. Inside the lobby, she asked the clerk where Slocum had gone. "On upstairs," the man said. "Room seven." June mounted the stairs, and in a short time she was knocking on the door of number seven.

"Who is it?" she heard Slocum ask.

"It's June, Slocum," she said. "Please let me in."

Slocum opened the door. "June," he said, "I didn't mean for that to happen out there."

"Oh, I know you didn't," she said. "Larry's just acting crazy. May I come in?"

"Oh, sure," said Slocum. "I'm sorry." He stepped back out of her way, and she walked on into the room. Slocum had left the door open deliberately, but June turned and shut it behind herself. Slocum awkwardly indicated a chair, and June sat down.

"June," he said, "I'm still on the job. I want you to know that. I don't mean you have to pay me, but I ain't quitting. That's all I mean."

"I know that," said June. "I just came up here to apologize for Larry's behavior. This business has just made him crazy. That's all. And then he listened to Pat, and—"

Slocum interrupted her. "Patton's the man we're after, June. I couldn't prove it in court, but I know it now. Patricia told me that her daddy was fixing to join her out in San Francisco just as soon as he got a big business deal finished up. He told her that he had a new man on the job who would clear it up in a hurry. Hell, that's got to be Marley. And that means that Marley's planning to do something real quick."

June sat forward anxiously in her chair. "Slocum," she said, "what will you do?"

"I'm tired of just sitting back and waiting," he said. "It's pretty clear what we've got to do. If Patton means to wind this business up real fast, he's got to communicate that to his man Marley. Somehow we've got to catch the two of them together. Spy on them if we can."

"We have to watch their every move then," said June.

"Yeah. That's right."

"They could be talking right now."

"I don't think so," Slocum said. "Patton has been real careful about acting like Marley is a stranger and nothing to him but a customer. He doesn't want to be seen talking to the man. I figure he'll wait till after dark."

"But how will we know when and where," June said, "and even then, how will we be able to spy on their conversation?"

"I sure haven't figured that one out yet," Slocum admitted.

June sat for a moment in deep thought, and then she said, "Maybe I can do something." Then she stood up. "I'd better be getting back to Larry," she said. Slocum jumped up to open the door for her, and she stepped in close to him, put both her arms around his shoulders and kissed him full on the lips. Slocum was astonished. June broke loose and without another word walked out of the room. Slocum stood rubbing his lips in amazement. When he was sure that he was absolutely alone again, he said out loud, "That damn stupid Larry Glover."

June knew that Broderick Marley was staying in a room at the Whistle Stop. She knew that the Whistle Stop, having once been a whorehouse, had a few rooms upstairs. She also knew that Patton did not often use the rooms, so it was some kind of special arrangement he had with Marley. And she knew that there was a set of outside stairs on the back side of the building. What she did not know was whether or not that outside door would be unlocked. She was thinking about these things as she made her way back to the store.

Inside, she found Larry still surly. He was taking a customer's money and making change, and he at least made an effort to be friendly to the customer. June moved behind the counter.

"Larry," she said, "take the rest of the day off if you want. I can handle things here."

"I'm all right," he said.

The door opened and Pat Patton stepped inside.

"Hello, Pat," said June, and she was afraid that her voice had been a little icy.

Patton tipped his hat and smiled. "Hi, June, how are you this fine day?"

"Doing nicely, thank you."

"Larry, you doing all right?"

"Yeah, Pat. Just fine. What can we do for you?"

"I need some pipe tobacco," Patton said. Larry turned to get it while Patton put his money on the counter. He had been a regular customer, so both Glovers knew his brand. "No trouble lately?" Patton asked.

"Not for a while," said Glover.

"Well, let's hope things hold up that way."

"Yeah."

"Pat," said June, "I didn't get a chance to say much to Patricia this morning, but she did say that she was off to San Francisco."

"Uh, yeah. That's right."

"Aren't you worried about her out there all alone?"

"Oh, no," Patton said. "I'm sending her to a nice hotel that's owned by a friend of mine. He'll look out for her till—"

June cocked her head. "Until . . . ?"

"Well, till I can join her out there," Patton said. "I've got a buyer for the Whistle Stop, and the deal ought to be concluded here in a few days."

"So you're leaving us?"

"Yeah, I'm afraid so."

"Oh, I wouldn't put it that way," June said. "San Francisco sounds awfully nice to me."

"Yeah. I guess so," said Patton with a shrug. "I, uh, I guess it's different for women. Now, me, I don't need much. I could be just as happy right here, but Patricia wants the latest fashions, nice restaurants, you know."

"Yes," said June. Patton made his excuses and left the store, and June turned on her husband. "Have you begun to put things together yet?" she asked.

"What do you mean?"

"Patton's getting out," she said. "He's already sent his daughter off."

"Well, he told us why," said Larry. "What's that got to do with anything? People move all the time."

"Larry, listen to me for once, will you? Pat's sent his daughter off early because he's looking for trouble. He's planning the trouble. Don't you see? If we had a daughter that age, would you send her off on a trip like that alone?"

"She'll be all right," Larry said. "Pat said she's going to a hotel that a friend of his owns."

"It's a long way from here to that hotel," said June. "Mark my words, Larry Glover, that Marley will be going into action just any time now."

"Marley?"

"Marley works for Patton."

"How'd you figure that? Did Slocum tell you that?"

June went through the motions of work for the rest of that day, but she was longing for nighttime. She had no other arguments for her stubborn husband. It was as if he just closed his ears or his brain or both. She wished that she could remember all the arguments that Slocum had used when he had explained it to her. It had made such sense to her, but she didn't seem to be able to present the argument as well to her husband. Well, she would just have to take things into her own hands. She surely couldn't leave them to Larry. If she did that, they would be ruined before they knew what was happening.

At last they closed the store, and Larry and June walked home. Once they got there, June began to ply Larry with whiskey. She knew that he'd already had a couple of drinks at the store. He was in the right mood for it. Ordinarily she wouldn't pour his whiskey. She didn't really care too much for his drinking. But this time she offered it each time she saw that his glass was getting low. Larry couldn't figure it out, but he didn't argue. It wasn't long before he passed out.

June changed her clothes into pants and a shirt. She walked out the back door of their house and looked around. It was a clear night, but she thought that it would be dark enough. She made her way through the alleys and back ways to the rear of the Whistle Stop. Hanging in the dark shadows, she looked around until she was sure that there was no one watching from any direction. Then she mounted the stairs that led up the back side of the building to the second floor.

On the landing, she looked around again. Then she tried the door. Surprised to find it unlocked, she opened it just a crack and peered in. Her heart almost stopped when she saw an inside door push open and Broderick Marley step out. She held her breath as Marley made his way down the short hallway to the landing of the inside stairs. Then he went down. June took a deep breath. She pushed the door open and walked in, stepping easy so as not to make any noise that might be heard downstairs. The Whistle Stop was busy, and the customers were noisy, so such precautions were hardly necessary.

June made her way to the room that Marley had just vacated and tried the door. It, too, was unlocked. Marley, being the only occupant of the upstairs, was probably not worried about anyone going in. She slipped quickly and quietly into the room. For a moment she just stood there trying to accustom her eyes to the light, or lack thereof, in the room. She saw some extra black clothes hanging on pegs on the wall. She saw a box of bullets on a table, and a water bowl and pitcher on another. Marley's rifle was leaning against the wall in a corner of the room. The bed was made. In fact, the entire room was neat. Marley was a neat man.

She couldn't see anything, though, that could possibly be of any help to her cause, and she was about to leave when she noticed that one of the small tables had a drawer. She moved to it quickly and opened the drawer, and there she found the letter. Taking it from the drawer, she moved to the window for better light. Even there, the light was not good for reading. She decided to take the letter with her. It was a bold move, but the times called for such things. She tucked it into her shirt and stepped back out into the hallway, closing the door easily. Then she heard footsteps on the stairs.

In a near panic, she looked toward the outside door she had come in through. It looked much farther away than it had on her way in. The footsteps were coming closer, and she could tell there were two sets of them. In desperation, she opened the door to the room next door to Marley's and stepped quickly inside. She pressed herself against the wall and tried to quiet her breath. It seemed as if it could be heard all the way down to the busy barroom. Out in the hall, the footsteps came closer. *What if they come into this room?* she thought. She waited, and then she heard the door to the room next door open. She prayed that Marley would not open the drawer to check on his letter. She listened as the door was shut behind Marley and whoever was with him. A girl, she thought. Probably just a girl. But then, the footsteps had sounded manly to her.

"Ain't you afraid someone might've seen us come up here together?" Marley said, and June was astonished to find that the voice came through the thin walls clearly.

"It's too late to worry about that anymore," came the answer, and June caught her breath. It was Pat Patton. No mistake about it. "We've got to conclude this deal right away."

"What do you want me to do?" Marley said.

"Kill Slocum for starts," Patton said. "Then do whatever it takes to get the Glovers out of that damn store. I've got to have that building."

"What's so important about that store?" Marley asked.

"I told you in my letter, didn't I, that there was a lot of money in this?"

"You did," said Marley. "How much are you talking about? Is it really a million?"

"Maybe more than a million."

"What? In that damn store?"

"It's buried underneath the store," Patton said. "It's the whole reason I moved to this town in the first place."

"How the hell did you find out about it?"

"I got the information from an old-timer on his death-bed," Patton said. "He'd been a Confederate soldier, and he was with a squad of men accompanying a gold shipment to somewhere or other. Somehow, they got word that the war had ended, and they didn't see any reason to let the Union get hold of the gold, so they buried it. Then they drew a map. Well, by the time this old bastard was dying, right in my own place of business, he was the only one left alive, and he had the map. He gave it to me, and I sold my business and moved here, only to find out that Glover's damn store had been built right on top of the damn gold."

"That sounds like a tall tale to me," said Marley.

"If it turns out to be not true," Patton said, "I'll still pay you for all your killing. If it is true, you're in for half."

"Half a million is a good chunk of change," Marley said.

"You could live like a king for the rest of your life."

"Yeah. Just for gunning Slocum."

"Well?" said Patton.

"I'll take care of Slocum tomorrow," Marley said. "What then?"

"I believe that once you get rid of Slocum," said Patton, "the Glovers will sell out to me."

"What if they don't?"

"Then we'll have to get rid of them, too. If it has to be that way, we'll just make them disappear, and I'll come up with a bill of sale for the store."

"And if they're gone," said Marley, "ain't no one likely to question it."

"That's right."

"All right, partner," Marley said, "we'll get it all done and wrapped up like a pretty Christmas present."

23

June was wondering just how long she would have to stay hidden in the empty one-time whore's room, how long it would be before someone would step into that room for some reason, or how long it would take for Marley to discover the theft of his letter. Even more important, she wondered how long it would be before the two crooks next door would hear the sounds of her heavy breathing through the thin walls. At last, though, she heard the sounds of their leaving the room and shutting the door behind them, their footsteps walking down the hallway, growing dimmer, and the beginning of their descent of the stairway. She waited another moment, hearing nothing but the sounds from the saloon downstairs, and then she slowly opened the door and peeped outside into the empty hallway.

Hurriedly, she left the room and walked as fast as she could to the outside door at the end of the hallway. Forcing herself to take her time, she opened the door just a crack and looked out. The alley was still deserted. She went out and down the stairs as fast as she could go. She knew that she would not be able to tell Larry about the evidence she had heard or show him the letter she had found. He would be out cold till sometime in the morning. She could not wait, though. She had to do something. She had to tell someone, and there was only one person. She hurried on down the alley until she had reached the back of the hotel. She slipped in the back door and inched along to the stairway. She looked toward the lobby and the counter. There was no one looking in her direction. Quickly she turned the corner and moved up the stairs. The hallway up there was empty, and June boldly knocked on Slocum's door.

"Who's there?"

"Open up," she said. "Hurry. It's June."

Slocum had the door open in a flash and June slipped quickly inside. This time Slocum shut the door behind her.

"June," he said, "what the hell—"

"Listen, Slocum," she said. "I've got it all." She went on to tell Slocum of her entire adventure. When she got to the part where she had stolen the letter, she reached inside her shirt and pulled it out, handing it to Slocum. She had not even read it herself. Slocum read the letter over hurriedly. "Well," she said, "what's it say?"

"Oh," Slocum said, "you haven't read it?"

"It was too dark," June said. "Read it out loud."

"Well, it's addressed to Broderick Marley, and it says, 'Mr. Marley, I'm grateful to our mutual friend, Ed Arlington, for getting me in touch with you. I have an important job for you. I've got to run a couple of storekeepers out of town. I hired some cowhands at cheap wages to do the job for me, but they failed miserably. I won't insult you with the same kind of offer I made to them. I'll pay you well. Half the cash. And there is a bundle, I assure you. As I told you before, there is at least a million dollars worth of gold involved. When you get to town, act like you don't know me. I'll get word to you somehow at the saloon.' It's signed, 'Pat Patton, Whistle Stop Saloon, Mesa Poquita.' Well, by God, June, I'd say this is all the proof we need."

"Just wait," she said. "There's more." She went on to detail the rest of her night's adventure, how she nearly got herself caught and hid in the next-door room, where she eavesdropped on the conversation between Patton and Marley. She told him everything the two men had said to one another. At last she sat down in the chair with a long and heavy sigh.

"June," said Slocum, "you might have got yourself killed. That was a damn fool thing you done." Then before she had a chance to respond, he added, "But it sure did work out good. You got exactly what we needed. Does Larry know about this?"

She shook her head. "Larry's dead drunk. I had to get him that way so I could get out of the house."

"Well, I guess it was the only way you could have dealt with him, under the circumstances."

She gave a little laugh and a shrug. Then she said, "Oh, God, Slocum, I was so scared."

"Well, that shows good sense," he said, "but it sounds to me like you done everything just right. And it's all over now, and you're okay."

"But it's not all over," she said. "What do we do now?"

Slocum looked at her. He knew what he would like to do at that moment all right, and he had half a mind to make his move. He fought the urge off as best he could. Wasn't it just his damn luck to finally run across one woman he thought he would really be able to love, could even settle down with, and she had to have her a damned husband. One as blind as Larry Glover at that.

"Go on home," he said. "When Larry wakes up in the morning, tell him the story. If you don't mind, I'll hang on to this." He held the purloined letter up for her to see. "I'd like to show it to the 'acting' sheriff. I'll get over to the store to see you and Larry first thing in the morning."

"Thanks, Slocum," she said, standing up. And again, to his everlasting amazement, she took him in her arms and kissed him, a tender and luscious kiss, and then she left. God damn, thought Slocum, I'd kill a man just for that kiss. He stepped out the door, shoving the letter into his shirt, and watched as June made her way down the stairs. A couple of minutes later he followed, but he did not go out the back way as she had done. He walked through the lobby and out the front door. Then he made straight for the sheriff's office.

He caught Pearly outside locking the door. "Hold it, Pearly," he said. "You ain't done yet."

Pearly looked over his shoulder to see Slocum. "Oh,

hell, Slocum," he said. "It's been a long day. You know, I'm the only son of a bitch in this office now."

"I know, Pearly," Slocum said. "Don't worry. I won't keep you long."

Pearly moaned and opened the door again. It was dark inside, and Slocum made Pearly light the lamp again. Pearly did so, complaining, and with the lamp lit, Slocum handed him the letter. As Pearly read, his jaw dropped, until by the time he had finished he looked as if he might be trying to catch flies.

"Now, Pearly," said Slocum, "I don't know what's going to happen tonight or in the morning, but it could be damn near anything. You get my meaning?"

"Yes, sir," Pearly said.

"The reason I bothered you with this tonight is that I want you to know just what the hell is going on before it even happens. You understand?"

"Yes, sir. Mr. Slocum?"

Slocum looked at Pearly.

"Mr. Slocum, what do you want me to do?"

"Nothing, Pearly. Just stay clear. Okay?"

"Yes sir. I'll do that all right. Be glad to. Thank you, Mr. Slocum. Thank you."

"You can lock up now, Pearly," said Slocum, and he took back the letter and walked out of the office. He did not look back. He walked straight to the Whistle Stop and bought a bottle of good whiskey. He saw Marley sitting again at his favorite table, and he gave the man a nod. Marley returned it. That was all. Slocum took his bottle and walked back to the hotel.

In his room, he poured himself a drink. Then he sat on the bed, leaning back against the wall, holding the drink in his hand. He knew that in the morning at the latest he would have to face Marley, one way or another. He was not afraid of Marley—at least, not much. Marley was good, though. Damn good. He knew that much about the man. Slocum was smart enough to realize that Marley could easily kill him if he wasn't really careful. He thought about Patton, too, but Patton would not be any trouble once Marley was out of the way. Hell, Slocum thought. Patton's only real problem was that he had created a spoiled daughter who was about to send her father straight to hell and didn't even know it. Likely she didn't care much either. Well, Patton had some cash, and if he really did sell the Whistle Stop right away, he'd have even more. Slocum had Patricia's San Francisco address. He'd see that the money was sent to her—if he was still alive to do so.

And Larry Glover. He was a nice enough guy. Slocum liked Glover all right. Glover just couldn't take the pressure, and Slocum guessed that he really couldn't blame the poor fellow. After all, he was just a storekeeper. He wasn't used to dealing with the kinds of trouble that had come his way. When he learned the truth in the morning, he would be insufferable, apologetic, ashamed. Slocum could hardly bear to think of facing Glover in that condition.

But what if there really was a million dollars in gold underneath the Glovers' store? What the hell would become of that? Could he just see to it that the Glovers kept it? He didn't think so. It would probably belong to the damned government, and like a fool, he realized, he had already let the deputy sheriff, the "acting sheriff," in on the knowledge. Even if he had not, it would be almost impossible to tear up the store to get at the stuff and not let the whole damn town in on the secret. It might be best, he thought, to just let on that the whole thing had been a great hoax that Patton had fallen for and then leave the damn stuff where it was—if it was really there.

But if they tore up the store and dug it up and there was really gold there, a million or more worth, and then they had to turn it in the U.S. government, there might be a reward for it. The Glovers would have that to put in the bank. That wouldn't be a bad deal for them, he thought.

He raised his glass at last and took a sip of the soothing whiskey, luxuriating in the feel of it burning its way down his throat and then warming his insides. It was good whiskey, and he appreciated it. He put the glass down on the table that stood beside the bed and took out a cigar from his pocket and lit it. Drawing deep on the smoke, he reflected that he was enjoying two of the greatest pleasures he knew. The third one—well, it seemed somewhat hollow just at that moment. He could think of only one woman in the whole world who mattered to him a bit just then, and she was way out of his reach.

He thought of the lovely and bold Mrs. Larry Glover—June. He thought of her and he longed for her. The memories of her kisses stayed with him, and he longed for more of them. He tried hard, but he could not think of one thing in the whole wide world that he would not do for that woman. He even imagined himself in Larry Glover's place, keeping a store. He would do that for June, if that was what she wanted of him. She was a wonder and a glory. He had never known another woman to match her, and he told himself that he knew he never would.

He drained his glass and reached for the bottle to pour himself another, and then he recalled what he had told Pearly. He did not know what might happen this night or in the morning. He knew that he would have to be ready, and that did not mean being drunk. Slocum knew how much he could drink without becoming impaired, but he wasn't at all sure that he wanted to stick to that limit on this night. Try as he might, he could not get the image of the marvelous June to leave him alone, and just behind it, always, came the image of the wretched Larry. Well, there was only one thing for it.

Slocum got up and jobbed a chair underneath the doorknob. Then he took off his gunbelt, removed the Colt from the holster, got back onto the bed and laid the Colt beside himself. He settled back to smoke his cigar and drink his whiskey and dream his sorrowful dreams.

Morning came early for Slocum. He had indulged himself perhaps a bit too much. He washed his face in cold water, and he dressed in clean clothes. Then he strapped his Colt on, checked it over and put on his hat. He walked out the door, down the stairs, out into the street and over to the eating place. He was ravenously hungry. A night of too much drinking always did that to him.

He was early, one of the place's first customers, and that was just fine with him. If there had been another place to eat, he would have gone there to avoid encountering Marley before he had eaten, or Larry Glover. He really did not look forward to seeing Larry.

He had his coffee in record time and was waiting for his order of eggs, ham, hash browns, biscuits and gravy, and wondering if he should have ordered some flapjacks to go with it all. He decided he could always do that later. He'd had three cups of coffee by the time his breakfast was served.

He was about halfway through with his meal when Pat Patton came in and nodded at him—nervously, Slocum thought. Slocum simply gave the man a cold look and kept eating. He finished his breakfast and ordered one more cup of coffee. He had just picked it up for his first sip when Larry and June came in together. Larry looked like something the dog had dragged in. He'd had a big drunk the night before, and it was obvious to Slocum that June had told him the tale of her adventure as well. There were great bags beneath Larry Glover's red eyes, and he walked like every step hurt. What hurt Slocum was the sight of June. She seemed more beautiful than he had remembered her.

They walked straight over to the table where Slocum was seated. God, he had been afraid they would do that. He shoved back his chair and stood until June was seated. Then he sat back down.

"Slocum," said Larry.

"Shut up, Larry," said Slocum. "I have an idea what you're fixing to say, or at least, what you're fixing to talk about, and I don't want to hear it. Not in here anyway." He turned and waved at the waiter. "Just get you some coffee and order some breakfast. We'll talk later."

Larry muttered something which Slocum took to be affirmative, and the waiter came over to the table. The Glovers ordered coffee and breakfasts. Slocum looked at June. "Did you tell him everything?" he asked.

"Yes," she said.

"Good," said Slocum. "Now he can read this."

He took the letter out of his shirt and handed it to June. She, in turn, handed it to Larry. He read it in silence and let it drop to the table. Slocum retrieved it and tucked it back into his shirt. He glanced over toward Patton and noticed that the man seemed to be looking at them with extra care. At Slocum's glance, he looked the other way. Slocum picked up his coffee cup and took another sip.

"If you two don't mind," he said, "I think I'll stick around while you eat. For some reason, I don't want to leave you alone today."

"You think today's the day?" said June in a low voice.

"If it don't come around of its own," said Slocum, "I'm just liable to bring it on in myself."

24

When the Glovers had finished their meals, Larry said to Slocum as he stood up, "I'm paying for all this." Slocum didn't argue. He waited till the two were outside before he got up to leave. The door was opened from the outside just as he reached it, and Slocum found himself face-to-face with Broderick Marley. He stepped aside, allowing Marley to enter. Marley stepped in and stopped, giving Slocum a hard look.

"Have a good breakfast," Slocum said. "It could be your last."

Marley smiled a half smile and saluted Slocum by touching the brim of his hat. Then he walked on in and found himself a table. Slocum went outside. Now he had a real problem. There was no longer any doubt as to who it was behind all the trouble the Glovers had been having, but that did not mean that Slocum could just go gunning for them. He strolled on over to the store and took up a seat on the sidewalk. It wasn't even a minute before Larry came out. His head was hanging.

"Slocum," he said, "I've been a fool. I—"

"Hold it right there, Larry," Slocum said. "I don't need to hear no apologies. I know what all you've been through, and it's enough to know that you've come to your senses."

"Thanks, Slocum," said Larry.

"Forget it. We've got plenty to think about just now."

"You think it's all coming to a head?"

"Almost any minute now," Slocum said. Just then he saw Patton and Marley both leave the eating place together and head for the Whistle Stop. Slocum nodded in their direction. "See there," he said. "They're out in the open now. It won't be long."

"What are you going to do?"

"I'm still thinking on it," Slocum said. "It might not be up to me."

The morning stage rolled into town just then, stopping at the station a ways down the street. Slocum watched as the passengers got off. One man, wearing a business suit and carrying a valise, stood on the sidewalk looking around. He spotted the Whistle Stop and walked directly toward it.

"That's interesting," Slocum said.

"Yeah," said Larry.

"Larry, why don't you run over to the sheriff's office and see if you can get ole Pearly to come over here?"

"Sure," Larry said, and he took off at a trot. Slocum kept watching the Whistle Stop. The man had gone inside. In another couple of minutes, Larry returned with Pearly.

"What is it, Mr. Slocum?" the acting sheriff asked.

"I'm just real curious about a stranger who came in on the stage," Slocum said. "I figured that you might could quiz him up without raising too much suspicion."

"Well, where is he?"

"He's in the Whistle Stop right now. He went straight to it."

"He must have a mighty dry throat," Pearly said.

"Could be."

"Hey, here he comes now," said Larry.

The man was moving toward the hotel. Pearly struck out on a line intended to intercept the man, and it worked. Slocum and Larry could hear the conversation that followed.

"Howdy," said Pearly.

"Hello."

"Just get into town?"

"I came on the stage."

"Being nosey is my business," Pearly said. "You see, I'm the sheriff here. You just passing through?"

"Well, yes, on this trip. I'll be back though. You see," the man withdrew paper from his pocket and handed it to Pearly, "I've just purchased the Whistle Stop. I'll be moving here permanently."

"Well, congratulations," Pearly said. "I wish you luck."

Slocum looked up at Larry.

"It sure looks like you were right," Larry said. "Patton's fixing to clear out."

"But not before he finishes up some other business."

"Yeah."

Pearly came walking back over to rejoin Slocum and Larry. "Well, he's just bought the Whistle Stop," he said. "He showed me the papers all right."

"Yeah," said Larry. "We could hear you over here."

"You know what that means, Pearly?" said Slocum.

"Yeah. Well, no. That is, I ain't exactly sure."

"What it means is that Patton and Marley are about to make their move on me and on Larry. Patton's got his business here all straightened out. He's ready to clear out of town, as soon as he finds a way to check on that gold underneath Larry's store. He's got nothing left to hold him here. If they pull something after dark, say, they could hightail it out of town without a worry."

"Yeah," said Pearly. "What should I do?"

"I don't know," said Slocum. "I'm just waiting for Marley to make a move on me."

"Say," said Larry, "I've got a thought."

Both other men looked at Larry, and Slocum said, "Well, let's hear it."

"Do we have enough evidence in that letter that June— well, that you got—to charge them with something? Conspiring together, for example. Anything?"

Slocum looked at Pearly.

"You got that letter on you?" Pearly asked.

Slocum pulled it out of his shirt and handed it to the sheriff, who reread it and studied it some, his face all scrunched up in deep thought. Finally he handed the letter back to Slocum. "Well," he said, "of course, I ain't no lawyer, but here's what it looks like to me. It looks like a trial could go either way, but it looks like there's sure enough suspicious things in that letter. Enough to maybe make a charge and arrest them and hold them for trial."

"I don't know about Patton," said Slocum, "but I don't think Marley'll stand still for being arrested."

"I'd hate to try to bring that man in," said Pearly.

"Slocum could do it," said Larry.

Slocum gave Larry a hard look.

"Yeah," said Pearly, a bit tentative.

"Well," said Larry, "you're the sheriff now, aren't you?"

"Uh, acting sheriff," Pearly admitted.

"Can't you appoint a deputy?"

"Well, I guess I could."

"Or two? Make me and Slocum deputies, and we'll go after the son of a bitches."

Pearly looked at Slocum. "Would you?" he said.

Slocum sighed heavily. "I don't want to wear no badge," he said, "and I don't want no appointment to last any longer than it has to."

"What do you say, Pearly?" said Larry. "Just temporary. No pay."

"Well, all right. I'll do it."

"I'll agree to it on one condition," said Slocum.

Pearly looked at him suspiciously. "What's that?" he asked.

"Just me. Leave Larry out of it."

"Now, wait a minute," Larry said.

"That's the deal," said Slocum. "Take it or leave it."

The newly appointed deputy, Slocum, walked into the Whistle Stop. He stepped to one side of the doorway and looked in on Patton and Marley sitting together at a table. Both men looked up at him.

"Slocum," said Patton, "what can I do for you?"

"You and your hired gunfighter there can come on over to the jail with me," said Slocum. "You're both under arrest for conspiracy."

Patton laughed a nervous laugh. "Conspiracy to do what?" he said.

"To raise hell with Larry and June Glover," said Slocum. "We know all about the gold you think is buried under their store, and we know that you've been behind all the trouble they've had lately. The latest thing you did is hire this cold-blooded bastard to come in and do your dirty work. You going to come along with me?"

"What authority do you have to make an arrest, Slocum?" asked Marley.

"I've just been appointed deputy sheriff," Slocum said.

"Where's your badge?"

"I don't need one."

Marley pushed back his chair slowly and stood up. Looking nervously from Slocum to Marley, Patton did the same, but when he got to his feet, he backed away from the table, winding up with his back to the bar.

"Slocum," said Marley, "I ain't going to no jail with you. I ain't going nowhere with you. You're going to have to shoot it out with me."

"I figured as much," said Slocum.

Marley took off the long black coat he was wearing, to expose his two Colts, and he hung the coat neatly on the back of a chair. Then he walked around the table. Patton eased his way along the bar toward the back of the room.

"Stand still, Patton," Slocum said. Patton stopped.

Pearly stepped through the front door just then and called out, "Hey, Slocum." Marley pulled his Colt, aiming at the door, and Pearly vanished outside again as Marley's bullet splintered a piece of doorjamb. Slocum's Colt was out in a flash, spitting lead. The first shot shattered Marley's right shoulder. The second tore into his chest. Marley staggered back, a look of astonishment on his face. He looked down at the blood pouring out over his chest and belly and down his right arm. He looked up at Slocum. Then he fell forward in a heap on the floor.

During all the excitement, Patton bolted for the back door. He was outside almost before Slocum knew he was gone. Slocum ran after him, slowing down only long enough to kick Marley's gun away from the body, just in case. He jerked open the back door, and then he stopped. Larry Glover had been waiting behind the Whistle Stop, and when Patton had come running out, Larry had caught him. Just as Slocum stepped out the door, Larry caught Patton on the side of the head with a roundhouse right, staggering him. Patton tried again to run, but Glover tackled him from behind. Then he stood up and, grabbing Patton by the coat collar, pulled him to his feet. He spun Patton around and belted him again. This blow knocked Patton to the alley on his back. Patton put both hands in front of his face.

"Don't," he said. "I give."

Pearly took Patton to jail, and Slocum and Larry headed for the store. Larry was grinning widely. Slocum looked at him and grinned, too. He understood Larry's exuberance. It was all over at last, and after so much frustration, it must have felt great to Larry to have landed the last punches of the battle. As they were about to step up onto the sidewalk in front of the store, June came out. Her face showed her anxiety and the questions that were in her mind. Slocum saved her the trouble of asking.

"It's all over," he said. "Marley's dead, and Larry beat Patton up and put him in jail."

Larry beamed with pride, and June ran to him and hugged him. While the Glovers were thus engaged, Slocum noticed a buggy coming into town. Thad Slater was driving and Millie was sitting beside him. Slocum walked back out into the street to meet them, and Thad halted the buggy.

"Hello, Slocum," he said.

"Hi," said Millie.

"What brings you two in?" Slocum asked.

"We're going to see the preacher," said Thad. "We got to line him up for our wedding. Now, don't go getting onto me for bringing Millie out while all this trouble is going on. We just couldn't wait no longer. Besides, I—"

"What trouble?" Slocum said. "There ain't no trouble here."

Millie looked astonished. "You mean—"

"It's all over with," said Slocum. "And congratulations to both of you."

As Thad drove on, Slocum walked back over to join the Glovers. Their embrace was over, but they were standing side by side with Larry's arm around June's shoulders. Both were smiling.

"Well," Slocum said, "when do you start tearing out the floor of your store?"

"We talked about that," said June, looking up at Larry.

"Yeah," said Larry. "You know, Patton was just chasing an old rumor. That's all. Why should we tear up a good store that's doing a good business just chasing a rumor?"

Slocum shook his head. "Well," he said, "I guess I can't answer that one."

Everyone had tried to talk Slocum into hanging around. The Glovers said he could work for them. Thad and Millie wanted him at their wedding. Old Sam Slater had offered Slocum a job. Even Pearly had suggested that Slocum stick around and run for sheriff. "Hell," he had said, "you'll get my vote." But Slocum had not really meant to hang around too long when he had first hit town. He thanked all of them kindly, wished them all the best of luck, saddled his Appaloosa and hit the trail. He had places to go and things to do. There were other towns on down the trail and other jobs along the way. He had— Hell, he might as well admit the truth. He just couldn't hang around any longer looking at June and knowing that she belonged to another man.

Watch for

SLOCUM AND THE CAYUSE SQUAW

301st novel in the exciting SLOCUM series
from Jove

Coming in March!